W9-CYU-510

ISBN 978-1-250-07971-8

9 781250 079718

5 0 7 9 9

THE CREATURE FROM MY CLOSET

POTTERWOOKIEE

Join Rob and the new creature from his closet in their hilarious dealings with **GIRLS, BULLIES, BOOKS**, and **MORE**.

OBERT SKYE

STAB-IN-THE-DARK

ARRG!

Praise for

WONKENSTEIN

THE CREATURE FROM MY CLOSET

"Quite funny and has a lot of laugh-out-loud moments. . . .
The idea of a hybrid Willy Wonka/Frankenstein character
is original and hilarious." —*School Library Journal*

"Highly amusing new series starter . . . Skye gives Rob a self-
deprecating charm and highlights the pleasures of books both
subtly and effectively." —*Booklist*

"Filled with spot-on commentary and a wince-inducing supporting
cast, middle grade guys won't be able to keep Wonkenstein to
themselves. . . . This pitch-perfect offering should appeal to
reluctant readers, not to mention the legion of Wimpy Kid fans."
—*Shelf Awareness*

"[A] fresh sense of wackiness." —*The Bulletin of the Center for
Children's Books*

"[C]omfy antics for readers who don't probably much like reading—
which, one thinks, is exactly the point." —*Kirkus Reviews*

POTTERWOOKIEE
THE CREATURE
FROM MY
CLOSET

OBERT SKYE

SQUARE
FISH

Christy Ottaviano Books

Henry Holt and Company + New York

SQUARE
FISH

An Imprint of Macmillan
175 Fifth Avenue
New York, NY 10010
mackids.com

Our books may be purchased in bulk for promotional, educational, or business
use. Please contact your local bookseller or the Macmillan Corporate and
Premium Sales Department at (800) 221-7945 ext. 5442 or by e-mail
at MacmillanSpecialMarkets@macmillan.com.

Library of Congress Cataloging-in-Publication Data
Skye, Obert.
Potterwookiee / Obert Skye.
p.   cm. — (Creature from my closet ; no. 2)
"Christy Ottaviano Books."
Summary: "The latest creature to emerge from Rob's closet is a cross
between Chewbacca from Star Wars and Harry Potter. Rob names him
'Potterwookiee' ('Hairy' for short) and soon Rob finds himself treading
water as he tries to figure out how to care for his mixed-up friend"—
Provided by publisher.
ISBN 978-1-250-07971-8 (paperback)   ISBN 978-0-8050-9753-5 (ebook)
[1. Monsters—Fiction. 2. Conduct of life—Fiction. 3. Books and reading—Fiction.
4. Schools—Fiction. 5. Family life—Fiction. 6. Humorous stories.] I. Title.
PZ7.S62877Pot 2012   [Fic]—dc23   2012011270

Originally published in the United States by Christy Ottaviano
Books/Henry Holt and Company, LLC
First Square Fish Edition: 2016
Book designed by Véronique Lefèvre Sweet
Square Fish logo designed by Filomena Tuosto

1 3 5 7 9 10 8 6 4 2

AR: 3.0 / LEXILE: 820L

For my brilliant Phoebe—
This book wouldn't be the same without you.

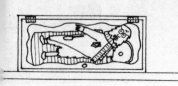

CONTENTS

POTTERWOOKIEE

THE CREATURE

FROM MY

CL☺SET

CHAPTER 1

~

PROBLEMS

My name is Robert Columbo Burnside, and I have a problem. There, I said it. Although I really should have said, "My name is Robert Columbo Burnside, and I have *a lot* of problems." For starters, I'm not completely sure how to begin this book.

ONCE UPON A CERTAIN TIME PERIOD...

NOT REALLY VERY FAR, FAR AWAY...

IT WAS THE BEST OF TIMES, IT WAS A WEEKDAY...

HERE COMES A BUNCH OF WORDS...

MY NAME IS ROBERT COLUMBO BURNSIDE, AND I HAVE A PROBLEM...

My sister, Libby, is another problem. She's
constantly obnoxious and usually staring at herself
in the mirror.

I'm also bothered by my younger brother, Kevin.
We call him Tuffin because when I was little I
couldn't pronounce his name right, so I said Tuffin.
The problem with him is that my mom insists on telling
everyone the story about his name. Two days ago, when
our new neighbor came over to borrow some sugar,
my mom went out of her way to embarrass me.

I think that's why parents were created, to embarrass us. Not that I don't like my mom and dad, but they're still a problem. I mean my mom calls me Ribert, and if she's not humiliating me, she's sleeping.

And my dad's a problem because he's constantly happy, even when things seem bad. He sells playground equipment to schools and cities, and he always wears a suit and tie. He loves his job.

My pets are sort of a problem. I have a fat dog named Puck, who whines and eats a lot, and a parrot named Fred. Fred escaped from his cage years ago, and we couldn't catch him. Now he just spends his days flying around the house and pooping on everything.

My friends are definitely a problem. For example, just last week we accidentally *broke* the photo booth at the mall, and my dad had to pay two hundred dollars to get it fixed.

I guess you're not supposed to have more than three people in the booth at a time. Now my dad has me cleaning things that don't need cleaning just to pay him back.

My neighbor Janae is a problem. Okay, she isn't really a problem, but her not being interested in me kind of is. We're on much better terms since the dramatic poetry contest. Still, whenever I see her, I feel like every joint in my body stops working, and I come unhinged.

I think one of my *biggest* problems is that I have to keep writing stuff down. It's not something I would normally do. I mean, to be completely honest . . .

It's also sort of a bummer that I'm not even getting a grade for all these words. It's like I'm doing an extra-credit project for no reason. Still, I know I have to document what is happening to me, because someday the world will need to know about the very biggest problem of all, MY CLOSET.

My closet used to be normal. It didn't have a door, and I used to sit inside of it and play with my homemade science lab. Then my dad found an old door at a garage sale. I think there's a good chance it's the heaviest door in the world—my arms get sore just opening it. It also has a gold doorknob with a small bearded man I call Beardy engraved on it.

I'm not sure I like Beardy; he's always looking at me weird. Once when I was gazing out my window and accidentally staring at Janae riding her bike with her friends, Beardy gave me a really smug look.

These days, however, Beardy's not the oddest thing about my closet. The oddest thing began a short

while ago when my mom forced me to clean my room.
To make the job easier, I just shoved everything into
my closet and shut the door. The new stuff mixed
with the old lab supplies and the many books my
mom was always giving me to read. A short while
later my closet began to make disturbing noises.

When my best friend, Trevor, and I tried to figure
out what was happening, we couldn't get the door open.
We tried to bust it down and pound off the knob,
but nothing worked. Finally it popped open on its

own, and there was Wonkenstein, a small, half Willy Wonka, half Frankenstein creature that caused me a lot of grief but also made things pretty exciting.

As soon as Wonk came out, my closet locked up. I tried everything to get it open, but Beardy kept it shut tight. I'm not positive what happens in there. My best guess is that all the lab supplies and all the books have begun to mingle. I think science chemicals are dripping down into the books and bringing mixed-up characters to life. I call it the Drip Theory.

Trevor calls it . . .

ONE MORE REASON TO BE WORRIED ABOUT YOUR FAMILY.

As soon as Wonk helped me solve my problem, he went back into the closet and disappeared. The only thing he left behind was his small cane, which I now keep on my dresser.

I thought that would be the end of the oddness, but soon after he left, my closet opened and I was visited by a new thing. Bits of him were hairy and fuzzy like Chewbacca the Wookiee from *Star Wars*. Other parts of him were sort of Harry Potterish. He's a little smaller than Wonkenstein, and he smells like a wet dog. He also showed up wearing a scarf, glasses, and a robe, and he was holding a wand. He has long hair over parts of his body. If I were a scientist I'd say . . .

Since I'm not a scientist, I decided to just call him something shorter—Hairy. He was friendly and interesting right from the start.

He's also my biggest problem at the moment. And as I was riding my bike to the library to do some research on him, I had a bad feeling that things were going to get worse before they got better. Hairy wiggled in my backpack. I thought about my dad and what he always says whenever he has a problem...

THE STICKY STUFF MAKES PEOPLE TOUGH!

If it's true, I think I'm about to become one of the stickiest kids around.

CHAPTER 2

STICKY FIRST STEP

I felt pretty good about heading to the library with Hairy. After all, libraries are famous for helping people.

As soon as we got to the library, I checked out the first volume of Harry Potter: *Harry Potter and the Sorcerer's Stone*. It was harder to choose a Star Wars book because there were so many. So I just picked the one based on my favorite movie, book four: *A New Hope*. My plan was to read about Hairy's different personalities, to really get to know the creature. I had seen the Harry Potter and Star Wars movies, but I had never read any of the books.

I found an empty table by the bathrooms and started to read. I was actually enjoying myself when I looked over and noticed that Hairy had crawled out of my backpack. He had also pulled a book off one of the shelves and eaten part of it.

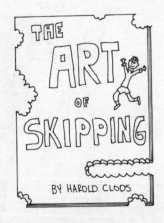

I pushed Hairy down into the backpack just as a librarian appeared out of nowhere. She saw the chewed-up book and screamed.

I wanted to tell her that Hairy ate the book, but I didn't want to freak her out, so I took the blame.

For some reason, the librarian was still freaked out. She agreed to let me off the hook if I paid an eight-dollar fine. I looked in my pockets.

I didn't have anywhere near that much money, so the librarian made me shelve books to work off my debt. It wouldn't have been too bad, except Hairy smelled and people kept looking at me like I was the stinky one.

While I was shelving a bunch of books about senior citizen vampires, I ran into my friend Jack. I'll be honest; I never thought I'd see him at the library. Of course before Wonkenstein, I never thought I'd see *me* at a library. Jack didn't look too happy about being spotted. He started rapidly making excuses for being there.

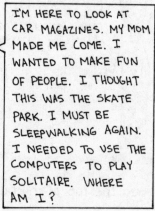

I'M HERE TO LOOK AT CAR MAGAZINES. MY MOM MADE ME COME. I WANTED TO MAKE FUN OF PEOPLE. I THOUGHT THIS WAS THE SKATE PARK. I MUST BE SLEEPWALKING AGAIN. I NEEDED TO USE THE COMPUTERS TO PLAY SOLITAIRE. WHERE AM I?

None of his excuses explained the books he was holding.

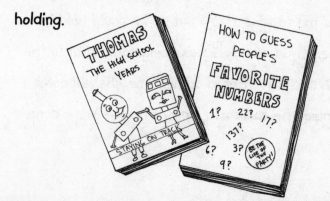

THOMAS THE HIGH SCHOOL YEARS

STAYING ON TRACK

HOW TO GUESS PEOPLE'S FAVORITE NUMBERS

1? 22?? 17?
131?
6? 3? BE THE LIFE OF THE PARTY!
9?

I didn't care why he was there, I was just glad to have someone to help me. I stood up and begged him nicely to stay and assist me while I worked off my fine.

I unzipped the top of my backpack and let Jack take a quick peek inside. He was pretty pleased to see that my closet had cooked up something new. He wanted me to take Hairy out so he could hold him, but there was no way I was going to do that in the library. So Jack offered to help me shelve books if I promised he could see Hairy when we were done.

After half an hour we got a little bored working so we started to straighten the books in a more creative way. It was sort of fun. Then a man wearing a hat and really short shorts told on us and ruined the whole thing.

Nobody arrested us, but the librarian made us go. As we were leaving, we walked past the community bulletin board near the exit. It was covered with announcements and ads from all sorts of local people and events. A poster in the lower right-hand corner caught my eye.

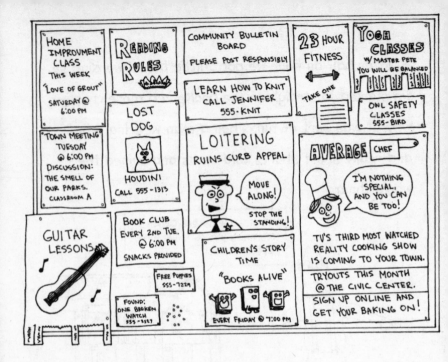

I couldn't believe it—*Average Chef* was one of my favorite shows on TV! It was hosted by a guy named Chad Average. Chad takes two teams of people and makes them race against each other to cook things using only eight average ingredients. One of those eight ingredients is chosen to be the focus of the meal, and the contestants have to make things that go along with it. The goal is to make the average food as interesting as possible. I once saw a man and his daughter make fish sticks out of pinto beans and dried macaroni. They also made sesame seed tartar sauce.

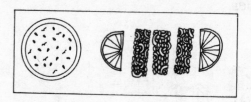

Now *Average Chef* was coming to my town for tryouts. I had problems, but I thought that if I made it to *Average Chef* and won the competition, Janae and girls everywhere might adore me. And I felt pretty confident that my problems would be less painful if I was adored.

When Jack and I finally got out of the library,
Wilt Johnson was sitting on my bike and cracking
his knuckles.

I thought about running away, but he was on my
bike. Besides, even if I ran, Wilt would find me. He was
a bully who thrived on bothering anyone smaller than
him. And since he was so huge, there weren't many
people he didn't bother. Once, when I was digging a
hole in the vacant lot with my friends, Wilt came by
and pushed us all in just so that he could, as he put it,
"see how many doofuses it takes to fill a hole."

Wilt loved to ride around the neighborhood on *bikes* he had "borrowed" and throw things at people. Now Wilt had *my* bike. The truth is, I was willing to walk the rest of my life if it meant he would take the bike and just leave me alone. Wilt told us to come closer, and like dumb robots, we mindlessly walked up to him.

Wilt informed me that he would *be* borrowing my bike for a while. I wanted to protest, but my urge to stay alive kept me quiet as he sat there resting his big rear on my seat.

There was no way I was going to let Wilt just take my bike. I *stood* up tall and looked him in the neck.

Thanks to my bravery, Wilt rode off on my bike and I was forced to walk home. Jack had his skateboard, but he decided to tag along with me. He was annoying as usual, and he kept begging me to let him see Hairy.

We cut across a large field, and when we got to the middle, I set my backpack down and took Hairy out. The little Potterwookiee stretched and growled and then began to walk around.

Hairy moved in an odd fashion. He took long steps, and his arms swung from side to side. He was so interesting to watch that Jack and I both temporarily forgot about the owls.

Okay, here's the deal. The city of Temon, where we live, has a secret—we have an owl problem. Well, I guess it's not a secret, but it's definitely not something you'll ever see printed in our tourist brochure.

Hundreds of screaming owls live in caves on the outskirts of town, and they eat mice and small animals. There are always stories in the paper about some huge owl picking up a tiny dog or a cat and carrying it off. My mom never used to let Tuffin play outside alone because she thought he might get taken by a bird. Then he kept interrupting her quiet time, so she changed her mind.

I never worry about owls picking up Tuffin, because he's too big. I also don't worry about them getting our dog, Puck, because he's too fat.

But now, as Hairy was dancing around in the field, an owl spotted him and swooped down. Jack and I screamed like those frightened women in scary movies.

The owl yelled back, and all of our screeching combined created a sort of sonic boom of fear.

The owl backpedaled in the air and took off in the other direction. Hairy waved his wand, yelled something, and then fell to the ground as if in a trance. I grabbed the little Potterwookiee and ran home as fast as I could. Jack wanted to stay and brush Hairy's hair, but I made him go.

I was mad about Wilt taking my bike and having to walk home, but the worst part was that Hairy was so scared he wouldn't talk or even move. I could feel my problems multiplying. I needed to tell my parents about Wilt taking my bike. I needed to tell them about Hairy and what was happening. Instead, I only told them the most important thing . . .

AVERAGE CHEF IS COMING TO TOWN !!

IS THAT THE SHOW ABOUT GYMNAST COOKS?

NO, THAT'S AGILE CHEF. THIS IS THE ONE WHERE NORMAL PEOPLE COOK.

My dad started talking about how educational
Average Chef was while my mom sniffed the air.

I went into my room, laid Hairy on my bed, and
took a shower. After my shower, I changed into my
pajamas. I always wore one of my dad's old concert
T-shirts to bed. He had tons of them, and they were
really comfortable. I then sat down on my beanbag
and started reading. It seemed like the next best step
to understanding why Hairy was here.

CHAPTER 3

~

FRIENDS

I read on my *beanbag* until my father came into my room and told me to turn off my light. He then repeated the *same* words he quoted every night.

EARLY TO BED AND EARLY TO RISE MAKES A MAN HEALTHY, WEALTHY, AND WISE!

I kept reading under my blanket with a flashlight until my mom came into my room and shared her own saying . . .

I then secretly read with the help of a glow stick and two blankets. It was really warm under those blankets and somewhere after midnight, my eyelids grew so heavy I could barely keep them open.

When I woke up the next morning, I realized that I had read over half of *The Sorcerer's Stone*. I guess caring for Wonkenstein had helped make me a much faster reader. Of course, it helped that the book I was reading was really good. It was way better than the movie. Also, I'm not sure if you're aware of this, and I really don't want to freak anybody out, but there are parts of the book that aren't even in the movie. I sort of feel like I should call the author and tell her.

HELLO, MS. ROWLING?

YES, LET ME SWITCH OFF THE HOOVER.*

TEAM HARRY

* VACUUM IN BRITISH-SPEAK

My guess is she probably already knows that so I've decided to hold off on calling her. I stretched

and looked around my room. I couldn't *see* Hairy
right off, but I could smell something.

I HOPE THAT'S NOT BREAKFAST.

Hairy had slipped down and under my bed. I pulled
him out and put him on my pillow.

I got dressed for the day and then spent a couple
seconds just looking at him. He was still not moving,
and he was staring into space as if in a trance. I'm
not a doctor or a hypnotist, so I don't know much
about trances. I do remember seeing a movie a few
years ago about a person who was under a spell. I
also remembered that the only way they got the

person out of her spell was to sing to her about love. I couldn't think of anything else to try, so I cleared my throat and gave it a go.

It was embarrassing, but I thought I saw one of Hairy's fingers twitch, so I kept going. I was just about to sing a second verse when someone knocked on my window and interrupted my performance.

I turned around and saw my friends' faces pushed up against the glass. I stopped singing and tried to make it look like I had been burping instead. I think they bought it.

LA, LA, LA......BELCH

My friends usually come in through my window instead of using our front door. It makes my mom mad. I figure I'm just doing her a favor by not having my friends ring the doorbell and traipse in dirt and other junk.

I shoved Hairy under my covers and opened the window. The second it was open, my friends came crashing in. They all started speaking at once.

Jack had told all of them about my Potterwookiee, and now they wanted to see if it was true. I tried to explain that Jack didn't know what he was talking about as Jack began sniffing around.

Jack howled and pointed toward my bed. They all began to tear through my blankets like a pack of wild dogs.

Jack set Hairy on the bed as everyone huddled around to get a closer look. Poor Hairy just lay there stiffly. I was actually kind of worried about him until his left eye closed and opened in a slow wink. Nobody else noticed because they were too busy making fun of me for sleeping with a stuffed animal. At first their taunting didn't bother me. Then they figured they might as well make fun of me for other things as well.

Apparently I was really easy to tease. They were wrong about one thing, though. Hairy was not a stuffed animal. Sure, I admit I like *Average Chef*, but that's because it involves food and TV, two of my favorite things. As for Thumb Buddies, none of my friends had any idea that I still collected them.

Thumb Buddies are my secret obsession. They were popular years ago. Then they stopped making them due to too many kids getting poked. Also, some parenting magazine called them "the worst idea for a toy ever!" I disagree. I love how small and detailed they are. I used to openly collect them, and now I have to secretly collect them through eBay and Thumb Buddies conventions. My friends would make fun of me forever if they knew what was in the bottom drawer of my dresser.

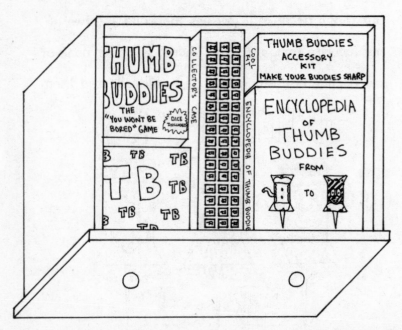

I scooted over and stood in front of my dresser, just to be safe. My friends weren't interested in my drawer. They were just annoyed with Jack for bringing them over to see a stuffed animal. Teddy punched Jack in the arm and called him a couple of names as they all turned to head back out of my window. I would have been safe, had Rourk not decided to open his dumb mouth.

Rourk is one of our friends, but he rarely makes things better when he talks. He likes to act tough, talk loud, and sometimes even swear. Of course, it isn't real swearing. He just repeats what he thinks he heard his older brother say. He usually hears it wrong in the first place, so his swear words don't make much sense.

My mom never lets me have sleepovers at Rourk's house, and I'm fine with that. Last time Aaron stayed at Rourk's, he had to sleep on the floor, and Rourk's older brother shaved the side of his head and stole his pants.

Now as my friends were getting ready to leave,
Rourk decided to open his bothersome mouth
and say . . .

I grabbed Hairy and backed away. I tried to
reason with them, but they had only one thing on
their minds. It looked like Hairy was headed for a
bit of trouble.

CHAPTER 4

THE FLINGER

Okay, now might *be* the perfect spot for a...

TIME-OUT!

I need to fill you in on something. In my neighborhood, there are alleys that run behind most of the houses.

Once a week, garbage trucks drive down them and collect the trash. The rest of the time, we use the alleys as shortcuts to travel around the neighborhood. A good thing about the alleys is the big trash cans. On occasion Trevor and I will go Dumpster diving and find cool stuff that other people have foolishly thrown away.

Three months ago, Trevor and I found a really big plastic plank. We had no idea what it was, but we knew it was definitely worth keeping. We carried the plank from the alley, and after making a few stops to test its strength, we brought it to the rock-covered island in the middle of our cul-de-sac.

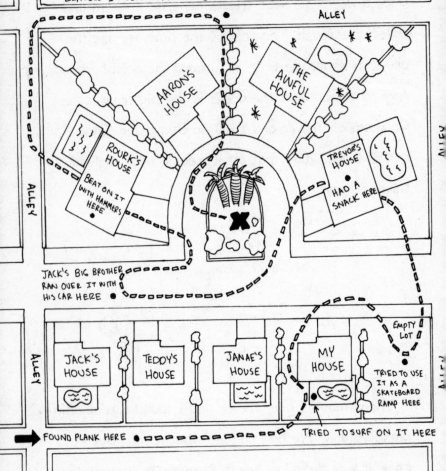

When we got to the island, we put the plastic

plank across a log. For some reason, we thought it

would make a really great seesaw.

It was too low and short to work as a seesaw, so we decided to turn it into a catapult. I taped a big bowl onto one end and then we moved it next to one of the big rocks on the island. Now all we have to do is leap off the jumping rock onto the other end of the plastic plank, and it flings stuff way up into the air.

After the stuff shoots up, we try to catch it as it comes down.

I GOT IT!

My friends and I have launched watermelons, apples, footballs, pretty much anything we think will go up and come down in an enjoyable way. The best thing the Flinger has flung up so far is a bunch of ice cream sandwiches. Jack took them from his freezer and peeled off the wrappers, and we launched dozens at a time. Jack ended up getting grounded for wasting food, and they were pretty hard to catch, but the damage they caused was tasty.

Rourk had to take two showers just to get all the ice cream and cookie parts out of his hair.

All right, sorry for the interruption. I just thought it might be a good idea to fill you in on the Flinger, seeing how it was about to cause Hairy some grief.

CHAPTER 5

TAKING SIDES

I stepped back farther, holding Hairy tightly. There was no way they were going to put him in the Flinger.

I was going to demand that everyone leave my room, but before I could make the demand, Jack lunged for Hairy. As I moved to avoid Jack, Teddy yanked Hairy from my hands. Teddy then leapt out my window with everyone squeezing out right after him.

I charged after my friends. I ran across the street and over to the rock island, where they were all gathering around the Flinger. Jack was on top of the jumping rock, Teddy was putting Hairy in the launch bowl, and Aaron had climbed up one of the crooked palm trees to get a better view.

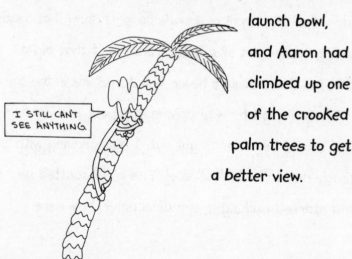

I didn't want to sound like a baby begging for his stuffed animal. Still, I had to help Hairy.

I was about to shove Teddy out of the way when a car pulled up in front of Janae's house. I know that a car pulling up in front of a house really isn't that big a deal, but it was Janae's house, and Janae was in the car.

The woman who was driving stopped, and Janae and two of her friends got out. I quit arguing with Teddy and tried to look cool. The girls spotted us and started walking in our direction. They were wearing tennis outfits and carrying rackets. I tried to be smooth and make a joke.

Janae smiled while her friends laughed. I felt like an idiot. I wanted to get on the Flinger and have someone fling me away. Teddy made me feel even dumber by filling them in on what was happening.

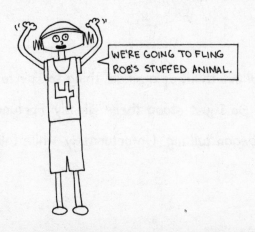

For some reason, Janae and her friends thought that was funny, too. Trevor tried to stick up for me, but it didn't help.

I was so embarrassed that my brain completely clocked out.

I couldn't think of a single thing to say to defend myself. So I just stood there silently. Fortunately, Janae began talking. Unfortunately, while talking, she informed us that she and her friends were going to be trying out for *Average Chef.* I had to say something, so my brain reluctantly clocked back in.

With my brain working again, I could feel words coming up my throat and pushing to get out of my mouth. I opened my mouth and blurted out . . .

Janae looked a little stunned. She stood there staring at me as if I had said something terrible. One of her friends pushed her aside and stepped closer to let us know how things would be.

It was nice of Trevor to step up, but none of my friends know how to cook. I did need help for the tryouts. It just didn't seem like they would want to participate in a cooking contest. I asked them if they were serious about helping me.

I told them "probably," and just like that, they were all in. Jack started talking about how famous he was going to be as Janae stepped closer. I thought she was going to whisper something encouraging, but instead she said . . .

I thought about pointing out to her how all great chefs were men, but then I remembered a bunch of women chefs who were great, too. Duh. I thought about telling her I would back out if she promised to like me. Jack, however, ruined the mood by jumping off the rock and onto the Flinger. He was tired of waiting to fling Hairy. Jack came down hard on the end of the catapult and sent Hairy skyrocketing straight into the air. I couldn't be sure, but it sounded like Hairy was muttering something.

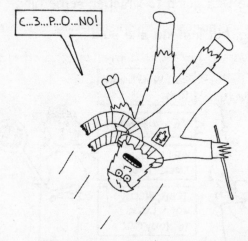

Hairy went flinging upward. I kept my eyes on him as he arched and then began to fall back down to earth. A breeze blew him to the right, and I had to run and then twist and dive to even make the catch.

I rolled over on the rocks and dirt of the island and came to a stop, wrapping myself around the palm tree Aaron was clinging to. Rocks were flying everywhere. I managed to shield Hairy so he wasn't harmed. Waving my right arm, I let the others know I was alive.

Nobody seemed that relieved. I stood up, dusted myself off, and then stormed back to my house with my Potterwookiee to pout in private. Everyone including Janae laughed as I walked away.

It wasn't unusual for my friends to laugh at me, but Janae and her friends had no right. I stomped into my house, put Hairy on my bed, and then went right to the computer. I had something to prove, and I wanted to make sure I would get the chance to do it.

I signed up for *Average Chef* online and then went to my room. I was irritated with my friends, and my head felt like it needed a distraction. As I set Hairy down on my pillow, one of his fingers twitched and pointed toward the books on my bed. As he twitched, he mumbled something that sounded like "hurry." He could have been saying "Murray," but that made no sense. I think he wanted me to hurry and read so that I could find a solution to his problem. I grabbed one of my books and dove in headfirst.

CHAPTER 6

TUCKED AWAY

After a couple hours of reading, I put my book down. I stared at Hairy as he lay there. I wanted to call Trevor over so we could discuss the little Potterwookiee, but I didn't want to leave Hairy alone, since our only phone was in the kitchen. Things would be different if I had a cell phone, or if I was allowed to lock my bedroom door. Of course, my mom won't let me do that. She always says...

A LOCKED DOOR IS AN OPEN PROBLEM.

In fact, checking to make sure that my bedroom door isn't locked is one of the few things my mom enjoys getting off the couch to do. She likes to know that my door is unlocked so she can go in and make sure I haven't done something horrible.

So with my door always unlocked, Tuffin was free to wander in and take Hairy. And while Tuffin wouldn't intentionally hurt Hairy, he was great at

shoving things in places they didn't belong. I
could only imagine where he might put the
Potterwookiee.

A LITTLE HELP, PLEASE.

I looked down at my purple beanbag, and a
possible solution popped into my head. I grabbed
the beanbag and unzipped it just enough to slip
Hairy into it. I pressed him into the soft white
foam balls and then zipped it back up. I left a
small opening at the end of the zipper so he could
peek out.

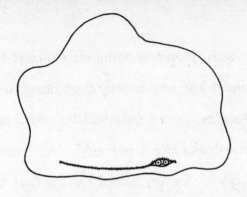

It was a perfect hiding place *because* Tuffin was scared of my *beanbag* and wouldn't go near it. Ever since he had watched the movie *The Blob*, he was afraid that my *beanbag* was going to eat him. Of course it didn't help that I told him some *beanbags* really did snack on people who sat on them.

I SHOULD NEVER HAVE SAT DOWN!

With Hairy hidden, I ran to the kitchen and called Trevor and told him to hurry over. Of all the kids I

hang out with, Trevor is definitely my best friend. He's a smart kid, who usually goes along with my plans. His glasses are constantly crooked, and his hair always looks like it is freshly cut. I share everything with Trevor, except for the fact that I still collect Thumb Buddies.

I went back into my room and unzipped the beanbag. I pulled Hairy out. He was covered in tiny foam balls.

It wasn't easy to clean Hairy off. When I was done, there were little foam balls all over my room. I was trying to sweep them up when Trevor arrived.

He crawled in through my bedroom window, and I gave Hairy to him so he could take a closer look. I explained how Hairy appeared to be part Harry Potter and part Wookiee and that I was calling him Hairy because it was shorter than Potterwookiee. I also told him how I believed that Hairy was under some sort of spell and we needed to break it.

MY DAD HAS A BOOK ABOUT MAGIC THAT MIGHT HELP. HE'S ALWAYS LOOKING FOR A SPELL TO GROW HIS HAIR BACK.

CAN WE BORROW HIS BOOK?

I CAN'T TAKE IT OUT OF MY HOUSE BECAUSE MY DAD SAID IT'S MORE VALUABLE THAN OUR FAMILY PHOTO ALBUM.

I had seen Trevor's family photo album, and it really wasn't that great. Trevor was an only child, and it was just a bunch of boring pictures of him standing in different places next to his dad.

"SUNNY DAY"   "BOYS' DAY OUT"   "SMILES"

I shoved Hairy back into my beanbag, and Trevor and I ran across the street to look at the book.

When we got to Trevor's house, his mom made us look at the magic book with her so that she could make sure we weren't getting our fingerprints all over it. It was filled with all kinds of cool facts about famous wizards. There was a large section about Harry Potter. Some facts were real, like what side of a broom you should get on to ride it—the left—and how to wash invisibility cloaks.

```
MACHINE WASH COLD WATER
INVISIBLE CYCLE
TUMBLE DRY MEDIUM HEAT
GOOD LUCK IRONING
```

We didn't get a chance to finish looking for answers, because I accidentally sneezed all over the book. You would have thought I had hurt a baby seal the way Trevor's mom was screaming. I tried to apologize, but she was too busy kicking us out of the house to hear me.

When we got back to my room, the beanbag was missing. I screamed, sounding a little like Trevor's mom. I thought Tuffin had taken it, but it turned out it was my mom. She had come to check if my door was locked, noticed the little foam balls all over my room, and decided to throw the beanbag away.

IT WAS OLD AND LEAKING STUFFING. I THREW IT OUT IN THE ALLEY TRASH CAN.

We ran out back as fast as we could. I knew it was trash day and we didn't have a moment to spare. The second we stepped out the back door, I could hear the garbage truck in the alley. I tore across my backyard and threw open the gate. What we saw made me want to pass out.

The beanbag was being tossed into the garbage truck! I ran out of the gate screaming, but the truck began to move quickly down the alley.

COME BACK WITH MY TRASH!

I could *see* the truck *stop* at the next house and lift the garbage can. After it *set* the can down, it began to close the back and compact the trash inside. Hairy was going to be crushed like a soda can!

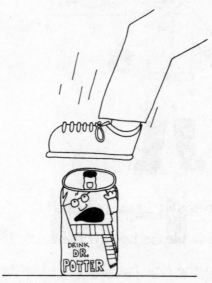

All at once, I reached down and picked up the biggest rock I could find. I heaved it as hard as I could. The rock hit the back of the metal truck and made a tremendously loud BONG!

The front door of the truck opened, and a big guy wearing a safety helmet and gloves got out and looked at me. He was holding a garbage stabber and breathing heavily.

I was scared, but I had to help Hairy. I pleaded with the man to please turn off the truck. He reached in and turned the key, causing the truck to hiss and then grow silent. The man yelled at me for throwing rocks, but when I explained that something important had been thrown away, he seemed to relax and understand my dilemma.

The man pressed a button, and the back of the truck hissed and opened. There, pressed into all the other trash, was my beanbag. It wasn't completely smashed, but I could tell that if it had gone two seconds longer, Hairy would have been more like a paper doll than a stuffed animal. The truck driver pulled out the beanbag and gave it to me like he was some sort of garbage Santa.

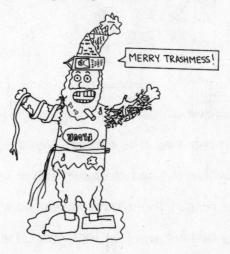

MERRY TRASHMESS!

Trevor and I thanked the garbage guy about a hundred times and then took the dirty beanbag back to my room. When I pulled Hairy out, he was slightly smooshed. Luckily, the white foam balls had kept him from getting hurt.

WE'RE LUCKY THAT HE'S OKAY.

YEAH, MAYBE YOU SHOULD KEEP HIM OUT OF THAT BEANBAG.

MAYBE WE SHOULD FIGURE OUT HOW TO BREAK THIS SPELL.

Hairy grunted as if he agreed. We carefully helped him straighten out and clean off. Trevor and I then spent the rest of the afternoon reading while Hairy lay on my bed not smelling that great. He did smile slightly, though, as he stared at the plastic glow-in-the-dark stars on my ceiling.

CHAPTER 7

FINDING SOLUTIONS

We read late into the night. Then Trevor went home,
and I read some more.

As the days went on, Hairy would mumble and twitch,
but he still spent most of his time
not moving. When we hang
out in my room, I just
read to him. I think he
likes it. I've been tearing
through the books about
him hoping to learn more.

I know that somewhere in the stories there's a permanent solution to Hairy's condition. Trevor has been reading, too. He read the entire Harry Potter series a long time ago, but now he's going through the books again, searching for the answer to get Hairy out of his spell.

THAT WORD SEEMS SUSPICIOUSLY OUT OF PLACE.

I finished the first volume of Harry Potter, and now I'm ten pages away from finishing the Star Wars book, *A New Hope*. My dad also claims it's the best because it was the first one made. I'm amazed by how much extra stuff is crammed into the books. My head feels like a Tetris game, filling up with bonus knowledge and information.

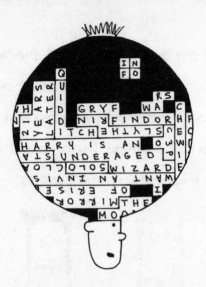

It seems like I'm reading all the time now. I even got busted at school yesterday for reading during class. I can honestly say that's never happened to me before.

BURNSIDE! STOP READING AND DO A PULL-UP.

SOFTROCK MIDDLE SCHOOL P.E.

Ever since the trash truck incident, I've been keeping Hairy safe and in my bottom dresser drawer. It was hard to do but I moved all my Thumb Buddies out into a hidden box in the garage. I worry about some of my more easily frightened Thumb Buddies.

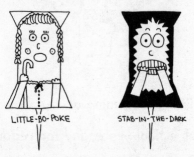

LITTLE-BO-POKE   STAB-IN-THE-DARK

So I now have an okay place to keep Hairy when I'm not in my room. The ongoing issue with him is that he stinks. My room smells awful. I'm starting to get a really bad reputation.

COME ON, RIBERT! THIS ISN'T A BARNYARD.

I've thought about taking him to school, but Principal Smelt would probably think the smell is me, and I'd get a lecture on hygiene.

SCRUB YOUR PITS, BUM, AND FEET, AND OTHER KIDS WILL THINK YOU'RE NEAT.

So, after coming home from school today, I decided to finally do something about Hairy's animal scent. I put Hairy and a bar of mint soap in my backpack and headed to the backyard. Libby was already out there, and she wasn't happy to see me.

IT'S MY TURN TO USE THE BACKYARD.

Libby was taking pictures of herself near the pool. She set up her camera and took shots of herself smelling flowers, suntanning, and tossing her hair. Libby claimed it's for some school art project, but I've never heard of one where you're assigned to make weird faces into a camera.

Libby insisted that I go back inside. I told her I had more important stuff to do than take pictures of myself, and she stormed off to tell on me.

I walked over to the back fence near a big metal tub and hose. I turned the hose on and began to fill up the basin we used to wash Puck in. I stood Hairy in the tub and let the water rise up around him. He didn't make a fuss because he couldn't move. I could tell from his expression, however, that he wasn't completely thrilled about the idea.

DON'T LOOK AT ME LIKE THAT. THIS IS FOR YOUR OWN GOOD.

I let the tub fill up and then splashed some water on his head and face. I soaped him up and was trying really hard to be careful, but as I turned him around, he slipped and went under. I had forgotten to bring a towel, so I pulled him out and hung him up in one of the trees to let the wind dry him off as the tub drained.

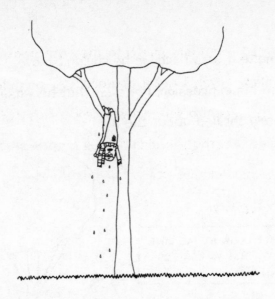

Sadly, there wasn't any wind, and I didn't have time
to wait for Hairy to dry out. So I set him in the now
empty tub and ran inside to get a blow-dryer.

Inside, my mom was opening the mail and
listening to Libby complain about me interrupting her
photo shoot.

I ignored them and snuck to the bathroom to get Libby's blow-dryer. I got it and grabbed an extension cord. I then spent a few minutes drying Hairy off. The good news was that he didn't smell bad anymore—in fact, he smelled sort of minty—but the drying had made him puffy.

It took a little while to shove him into my backpack because of how fluffy he'd gotten.

SORRY, THIS IS JUST UNTIL I GET YOU INSIDE.

Hairy was silent, but I heard a strange noise coming from the other side of the fence. There was the rustling of leaves as something moved around in Janae's front yard. My heart almost passed out. I could see something gazing back at me from one of the spaces at the top of the wall.

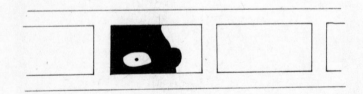

Someone was watching me.

CHAPTER 8

SAVED BY THE BELLE

The eye quickly disappeared, but I could hear whatever it was moving around on the other side of the fence.

I flung my backpack over my shoulder and ran across the yard. With a tug, I yanked open the back door and raced through my house. I placed my backpack behind the couch and dashed out the front door.

I ran through my front yard toward Janae's house. When I got to the side of her driveway, nobody was there.

I pretended for a second that it had just been Janae looking at me. I mean, maybe she likes me and just wants to get a secret glimpse.

Sadly, I knew that wasn't the case—the eyeball had been much bigger than Janae's. In fact, if she really were that big and scary, I don't think I would feel the same way I do about her.

I ran over to Trevor's house to tell him about the eye. As I was running up to his front door, Trevor sprang out and we collided.

We both went down hard. I twisted my right leg, and Trevor's glasses flew off and hit the ground. To make things worse, as I was getting up, I stepped on them.

Trevor picked up his broken glasses, told me to hold on, and then went back inside. When he came out again, he was wearing his scratched and ugly backup pair.

I was familiar with Trevor's backup glasses. He had worn them a short while last year after he had sneezed so hard that his regular glasses flew off and into the street, where a car drove over them.

The reason Trevor had been running out the door was because he thought he had figured out how to get Hairy to snap out of the spell. When Trevor asked me why I had been running, I told him about the strange eye staring at me through the wall.

WAS IT JANAE?

THAT'S WHAT I THOUGHT, BUT NO.

The eye story made Trevor a little uneasy. Trevor liked mysteries and excitement, but he preferred them to come in book form. A strange peeper peeping into my backyard felt like the beginning of something sinister.

We returned to my backyard, and I showed him where the eye had been spying on me. As I was talking I heard the noise again.

I normally wouldn't be freaked out because I don't really believe in things like zombies, but it wasn't very long ago that I didn't believe in creatures like Wonkenstein and Potterwookiee either.

The sound of someone moving along the outside of the wall grew louder. The noise stopped, and both Trevor and I held our breath. We could hear a scraping noise and then a dark shadow rose up over the back wall and jumped down. It was Wilt.

HELLO, DUMBO.

Wilt loved to call me Dumbo. Years ago he discovered that my middle name was Columbo. And since Dumbo rhymed so well, that's what he usually called me.

Wilt punched his fist into his palm and growled. Even though it was my yard, I felt like I had just been busted and now needed an excuse to be out there.

Even Wilt wasn't dense enough to buy that excuse. Trevor told him we were playing hide-and-seek and then closed his eyes and began to count.

Unfortunately, when Trevor opened his eyes, Wilt was still there.

Wilt stepped closer to both of us and looked me in the eye. I tried not to shake, but I was so nervous my hands were sweating.

I looked over at Trevor in his backup glasses. Amazingly, he wasn't frightened of Wilt. His mom and dad had taught him all sorts of things about personal safety and being cautious. If he were an action figure, he'd be something boring like...

Trevor didn't fear bullies. His mom had always told him that they were nothing but...

So Trevor wasn't scared, and he was now saying things to Wilt that sounded just like his mom.

YOU WEREN'T INVITED TO BE BACK HERE. AND JUST SO YOU KNOW, ROB WANTS HIS BIKE BACK OR HE'S GOING TO TELL HIS MOTHER.

I put my hands over my face and wished I were dead. I couldn't even look because I was scared Trevor might be trying to hug Wilt.

Wilt said something about how I had actually "given" my bike to him. He then demanded to know what we were being so secretive about back here.

NOTHING. WELL, SOMETHING, BUT IT'S NONE OF YOUR BEESWAX.

Once again, Trevor was messing things up. Plus, his backup glasses made it hard to take him seriously. Wilt stepped closer and punched his right fist into his left palm. For a second, I thought about just beating myself up to get it over with. Wilt opened his mouth, laughed, and then said to me...

I'M GOING TO REARRANGE YOUR FACE TO LOOK LIKE A MOUTHFUL OF CHEWED-UP BACON AND EGGS.

I suddenly wished I had a lightsaber. Wilt probably would have made good on his threat if it hadn't been for my sister. Libby came out into the yard to get her camera and pictures. She didn't know Wilt, so naturally she assumed he was a thief who was there to steal the pictures she had taken of herself.

PICTURE SNATCHER!

Wilt wanted nothing to do with Libby and her screaming. He scrambled back over the fence. Libby grabbed her stuff and stormed inside without saying another word. And just like that, Trevor and I were alone again.

THAT WORKED OUT WEIRD.

YEAH.

I NEVER THOUGHT I'D BE GLAD TO SEE LIBBY.

AND I WAS JUST ABOUT TO HUG HIM.

We went inside, and I retrieved my backpack from behind the couch. Both of us then went into the garage. Trevor filled me in about the "undoing" spell he had found in Harry Potter. It was in the first book, and I was mad that I hadn't spotted it myself. I propped Hairy up on my dad's old golf clubs, took his wand from his hand, and repeated the words Trevor thought would work.

FINITE INCANTATEM!

The tip of Hairy's little wand burned red, and a small spark shot out. Hairy started to shake, and his eyes blinked and rolled back into his head. His feet jiggled and then, while belching, his body jerked upward. He jumped down off of the golf clubs and wiggled his arms.

Trevor and I clapped and cheered. I thought Hairy was going to thank us for freeing him, but instead he said...

Hairy also made a few remarks about how dumb a hiding place the beanbag had been. I apologized, and Hairy explained how he had accidentally put himself under the spell while trying to fight off that owl. I apologized a second time for not being a better reader and figuring out how to free him sooner.

The three of us hung out in my bedroom for the rest of the afternoon. Hairy really wanted to know what house he was in. When I told him "mine," he laughed. It turned out he was talking about a different kind of house, the kind you'd find at Hogwarts. Well, that would take a sorting hat, and since I didn't have a real sorting hat, I had to improvise.

THE HAT SAYS YOU ARE IN THE REPUBLIC OF GRYFFINDOR.

NICE.

Trevor was pretty pleased that Hairy was there.
He had liked Wonkenstein, but he seemed even
more fascinated with Hairy. There was something
odd and almost hypnotizing about the creature. The
way he moved and spoke was cool. While we were
studying him, my mom knocked on my bedroom
door. Trevor shoved Hairy up the front of his shirt
to keep him hidden.

Mom opened the door and stared at Trevor. She
seemed more interested in his ugly glasses than in
what was under his shirt. She informed me she was
taking Libby and Tuffin shopping.

My mom stared at us and looked like she wanted to say something, but instead just shook her head. Trevor's stomach growled.

My mom told us there was bread in the bread box and suggested we make some sandwiches.

Trevor and I watched out my bedroom window until we saw her drive off with my brother and sister. Trevor took Hairy from under his shirt and handed him to me. Hairy hung on my arm smiling.

It was not the smartest question to ask, seeing
as how I knew he hadn't eaten anything for a while.
Hairy made me feel better by asking Trevor
something stupid.

Trevor explained his glasses as we all headed to
the kitchen to make something to eat.

I had never met Trevor's aunt, but if those had been her glasses, she probably wasn't.

CHAPTER 9

MAKING PLANS

I brought Hairy out into the kitchen and set him on
the counter. I wasn't worried about my mom coming
back soon. Whenever she and Libby went shopping,
it usually took hours. I also wasn't concerned about
my dad popping in. He hardly ever came home early
from work. And even when he did, he always—and I
mean always—honked the horn twice before turning
off his car. He says that "beep beep" in car language
means . . . I'M HOME!

There had *been* only a few times in my life that I could remember when my dad had not double-tapped the car horn when pulling up to our house. One of those times had *been* when they brought Tuffin back from *being* born, and the other had *been* when I was eight. My dad had just gone through a particularly bad parent-teacher conference with my teacher.

YOUR SON HAS A PROBLEM WITH EATING CHALK AND THEN BLOWING IT ALL OVER.

IS THAT NORMAL?

NO.

I guess my dad had *been* a little too concerned to honk when we got home. But I had gotten over my chalk problem, and I couldn't remember a time since then that he hadn't double-tapped upon arrival.

I fixed Hairy a peanut butter and ham sandwich as Trevor talked about what we were going to do for our *Average Chef* tryout.

We had talked with our friends earlier about what they wanted. Jack thought we should make spicy pancakes with some actual explosives in them. Aaron wanted whatever we made to have cheese. Rourk thought our meal should include a toy, and Teddy believed that whatever we cooked up would be a joke if it wasn't...

...CRUNCHY, STICKY, AND SORTA ROUND.

I had tried to explain to them that all we needed were a few basic recipes that we could use with whatever the average ingredients ended up being. I had seen the show enough times to know how it worked. So Trevor and I had gotten some good recipes out of my mom's cookbooks. My friends had come over yesterday, and we had practiced cooking a few things. It had gone pretty well. Still, the tryouts were in two days, and I needed to improve my cooking skills. Hairy was more than willing to help.

MAY I BE OF ASSISTANCE?

I loved when the Potter part of Hairy spoke. He had such a cool British accent. It made everything sound much more important than it was. Not that the Chewbacca part of him wasn't just as interesting. When I set him down in the Kitchen, he jumped up into the curtain and began shooting marshmallows at Puck.

TAKE THAT, JABBA!

I pulled him down and gave him one of the recipes. He read it aloud so we Knew what we were supposed to do. He was pretty helpful, but sometimes we couldn't understand him at all.

It felt great to be in the kitchen preparing for *Average Chef* and hanging out with a Potterwookiee. I still missed Wonk, but having Hairy made things a lot better. In between his telling us what to do, we would ask Hairy questions about himself and why he was here. He didn't have too many answers, but he kept saying . . .

Our cooking started to get a little messy, so we put on a couple of my mom's aprons. I even found a small one from one of Libby's old dolls for Hairy to use. We mixed all the ingredients together in a big casserole dish and put the food in the refrigerator. The doorbell rang.

I hid Hairy in the bread box and answered the door. It was Jack and Aaron. They were standing there looking stunned.

Judging by their hair, I could tell that both of them had recently been talking to Wilt. Wilt loved to lick his hand, smack your forehead, and then swirl it around your head until the front of your hair looked like a stringy bird's nest. He always pretended he was just fixing your hair, but we all knew better.

HERE, LET ME FIX THAT FOR YOU.

The worst part about Wilt-Whirls were that they were almost impossible to comb out. One kid at my school had to shave the middle of his hair just to correct what Wilt had done. It was like a reverse Mohawk.

AT LEAST YOU HAVE YOUR HEALTH.

Jack and Aaron came into the house and sat down at the dining room table. Both of them had such long hair to begin with that their whirls looked higher than any I had seen before. I asked them what had happened.

Aaron told us how Jack had spilled the beans. He said Jack had told Wilt about my closet and how I was probably hiding a creature of some sort.

Jack said that Wilt wanted me to meet him at Temon Cemetery tonight in the clearing by the single tree. He said I was supposed to bring Hairy and that if I did, I would get my *bike* back and avoid being beaten up.

I was so mad at Jack for ratting me out. I also thought it was weird that Wilt wanted to meet at the cemetery. Trevor cleared things up by reminding me that Wilt's dad was the caretaker and that they lived in a house on the back edge of the cemetery. I wasn't sure what to do. Trevor suggested . . .

WE SHOULD TELL OUR PARENTS.

I looked at Trevor and shook my head—we needed to handle this ourselves. I figured if I got all my friends, it would be six against one, and together we could take Wilt down. Believe it or not, Trevor,

Jack, and Aaron seemed to think this was a good idea. We all headed out to the island to fetch Rourk and Teddy and see if we could come up with a plan for getting my bike back and teaching Wilt a lesson. I was so mad and so pumped up that I forgot I had left Hairy hidden in the bread box.

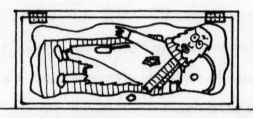

On the island we brainstormed and came up with a way to get my bike back and not get beaten up. We would surprise Wilt, quickly wrap him around the single tree in the cemetery, and then grab my bike.

After going over all the details, we saw my dad drive up the street and pull into my driveway. He double-tapped the horn and got out.

I waved across the street at him and then turned
my attention back to my friends. My dad went into
the house to make his afternoon snack and relax
after a hard day.

CHAPTER 10

THINGS

Our idea to get my *bike back* wasn't perfect, but we really hoped it would work. I was so nervous and excited that I was buzzing.

The second I stepped back into my house, however, my brain handed me a reminder.

Hairy! I ran to the bread box and threw it open. He wasn't there. I dashed around the kitchen, frantically throwing open cabinets and drawers. Nothing. I could hear the TV on in the family room, and when I looked around the corner, there was my dad sitting on his favorite chair and eating the last bite of a sandwich while watching one of his shows.

There was no way my dad could have gotten bread without seeing Hairy. I stepped in front of the TV.

My dad's eyes lit up.

For some reason, my dad loved it when his kids wondered. He always hoped that we were wondering about grand things like the universe or playground equipment. Of course, he was usually let down when the things we were wondering about weren't quite that important.

SO I WAS WONDERING, HOW WAS YOUR SANDWICH?

My dad looked pretty disappointed. He reported on his sandwich but didn't say anything about having seen a small creature in the bread box. I asked him if there was anything besides bread in the bread box.

LIKE BAGELS?

I shook my head and asked him if there had been anything besides bread or bagels. He said that the only other thing in there had been one of Tuffin's stuffed animals. He added that he had taken the stuffed animal out and tossed it into Tuffin's room.

THAT CHILD SHOVES THINGS INTO THE MOST INTERESTING PLACES.

I was too busy running to Tuffin's room to wonder about Tuffin's shoving habits. I groaned, worrying about Hairy and how messy Tuffin's room was. My little brother hates it when people touch his stuff. He won't even let my mom clean his room. He stacks everything he owns in piles and covers most of the piles with blankets and sheets to make it look like a mountain range.

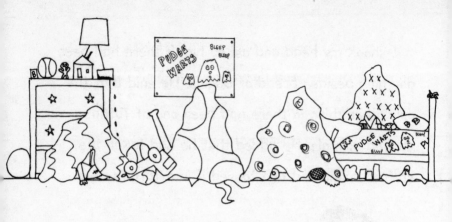

I knew that if Hairy had been thrown into Tuffin's room, there was a good chance that he was now uncomfortable and disoriented. I pushed open Tuffin's door, expecting the worst.

Hairy wasn't lost or disoriented. He was standing on a pile of junk and doing some sort of spell. Tuffin's toys and blankets were flying around the room. I stepped in and quickly closed the door as a plastic dragon flew by me followed by a toy Millennium Falcon. Hairy was smiling and chanting something in Latin. I looked on in awe until a basketball slammed me in the face.

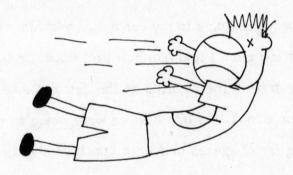

I tumbled and fell backward, landing on Hairy. Everything dropped to the ground as the two of us rolled down one of Tuffin's junk piles.

I brought Hairy to my room and told him all about our plan. I told him how Wilt would *be* by the single tree in the clearing at the Temon Cemetery at nine p.m. I told him how we were going to wear robes for disguises and tie a bunch of sheets together to make a long rope. I told him how when Wilt showed up, Rourk would signal with a duck call, and we would run around the tree and wrap him up it so that I could take my bike back.

Hairy spotted a problem—if Wilt didn't bring my

bike to the tree, then I still wouldn't have it. I smiled and told Hairy how seeing him fly those things around Tuffin's room had given me an idea.

I didn't want to bring Hairy with me, but it seemed like he was just what we needed. I explained my new idea to Hairy, and he asked me all kinds of questions about Wilt. He was confused at first. Then I told him that Wilt probably would have been in Slytherin or fighting with the Empire, and he seemed to understand. I explained bullies and how it was necessary for us to teach Wilt a lesson because he made everyone miserable.

Hairy seemed incredibly willing to help.

FOR MUGGLES EVERYWHERE!

Hairy and I talked until my mom came home and called me to come to dinner. I put Hairy into my pillow to keep him hidden while I ate.

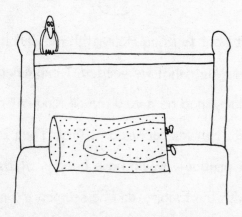

For dinner my mom had brought home tacos from a fast food place. The food was pretty good, but the conversation was painful. My mom and dad kept insisting that I include Tuffin on my team for the

Average Chef tryouts. They kept trying to convince me that he had some really good ideas. I politely told them no way.

NO, THANK YOU, PLEASE.

I also tried to explain that Tuffin was too young. I thought I had them with that argument, but then, Libby ruined it.

WASN'T THERE A FIVE-YEAR-OLD WHO WON *AVERAGE CHEF* ONCE? THAT'S YOUNGER THAN TUFFIN.

She was right, but the five-year-old had been a supergenius from New York who was raised by chefs and lived in an old restaurant that was supposedly haunted by other dead famous chefs. I tried a different argument.

I needed a sister more noble and supportive, like Princess Leia. Libby was making things awful. I wanted to fling taco meat at her like a monkey flings its waste.

I knew, however, that I needed to play it cool. There was no way I was going to include Tuffin, but if I was too mean about it, I might not be able to go out later tonight to take on Wilt. I tried to look pathetic and sad to get some sympathy.

THESE TRYOUTS ARE JUST SO IMPORTANT TO MY FRIENDS. I DON'T WANT TO RUIN THINGS.

My dad was falling for it, but my mom wasn't so sure. She tried one last time to guilt me into saying yes.

> I GUESS YOUR LITTLE BROTHER WILL JUST HAVE TO LIVE WITH A BROKEN HEART, THEN.

I told her how sorry I was, but that this might be okay, seeing as how sometimes life is hard and this probably was a good lesson for Tuffin to learn. Tuffin didn't look very grateful at all.

After rinsing off my plate, I went to my room. Hairy was still in my pillowcase, talking to himself about casting a spell on Darth Vader. We went over the plan again and what his small role might be tonight.

I SHALL NOT LET MY FEARS BROWN THE ENEMY'S TOAST.

Hairy was beginning to sound more and more like Dumbledore from *Harry Potter*. He would say wise things, but they were never quite right.

THERE IS WISDOM IN THE SNEEZE OF A STRANGER.

I didn't care—I liked Hairy a lot. In fact, I was beginning to hope that my closet would never open again and that Hairy might hang around for good. I glanced over at Beardy. I think he was listening to what Hairy and I had been talking about.

I was hoping that the smile on his face meant he approved of our plan.

CHAPTER 11

THE GRAVEYARD

At eight o'clock on the dot, the doorbell rang. I was sitting on my beanbag reading and pretending to be studious. Hairy was already in my backpack, along with the other supplies I would need.

I heard my mom get the front door, and I continued to act like I was reading. I was nervous about tonight, but I knew we needed to stop Wilt once and for all. A few moments later, my mom came into my room.

The first part of our plan was genius and failproof. Trevor knew there was going to be a full moon tonight, so he had told my mom that we needed to study it and write a report. I pretended like I didn't want to go, and that was all my mom needed to insist that I had to—she loves making me do homework.

I threw on my backpack and walked quickly to the front door. Trevor was standing on the sidewalk with a small telescope and his science book. I was happy to see that someone had fixed his regular glasses. They were still crooked on him, but at least he looked normal again.

Once we were out in the front yard, Trevor whistled and the rest of our friends popped up from behind the bushes. We were all supposed to bring something we could use to protect ourselves. Jack had his assault flashlight, Teddy had soap-on-a-rope that he was swinging around like a mace, Aaron had a flyswatter, and Rourk was wearing gloves that he thought gave him a super grip. Trevor's weapon was the pair of steel-toed boots he had borrowed from his dad. Me? I had my Nerf crossbow. Altogether, we made a pretty impressive team.

The full moon was *so* big it looked like we could reach out and touch it. Its light made it very easy to see things. Hairy growled softly in my backpack, and Jack thought it was me.

Rourk was an expert on eating, but as all six of us began to run to Temon Cemetery, Rourk's love of eating seemed to be having a negative effect on him.

Rourk kept begging us to slow down. By the time we got to the cemetery, he was so far behind, none of us could see him.

DO YOU THINK HE'S STILL COMING?

LAST I HEARD HIM, HE WAS SCREAMING SOMETHING ABOUT INTESTINAL CRAMPS.

After a few minutes, he caught up, limping and breathing wildly. We all had to wait for him to calm down before we could continue.

The main gate to Temon City Cemetery was locked, forcing us to climb over the ivy-covered wall. Once inside the wall, all of us pulled out bathrobes from our backpacks and put them on as disguises.

I had borrowed my dad's robe, but Teddy had borrowed his mom's, and Jack seemed to be wearing his grandma's. Trevor's robe was normal, but Aaron's was a big thermal thing with a long zipper down the front, and Rourk was wearing a huge T-shirt pulled up over his head.

We walked carefully to the clearing and the single tall tree. We then reached into our backpacks and pulled out bedsheets. All of us had brought plain sheets except for Jack.

Trevor tied the sheets together using a knot he had learned in Scouts. We then stretched them out across the clearing. Jack held one end while Trevor held the other.

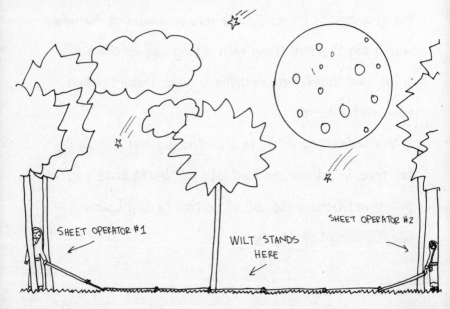

The rest of us moved into different places to wait for our part. Once I was alone, I took off my backpack and unzipped it. Hairy crawled out and shook. He still smelled like mint, and he was smiling. He seemed pretty taken with my bathrobe.

I pulled out the extra sheet I had packed and laid it on the ground. Hairy pointed his wand and then said a few words. The end of his wand glowed slightly, and the sheet began to rise.

The sheet hovered like a magic carpet for a few seconds before Hairy let it drop softly to the ground. We then crouched low and waited for Rourk to blow the duck call.

The night was full of strange noises, and the headstones made it seem like at any moment, zombies could show up. There were falling stars dropping from the sky.

It seemed like forever before I heard rustling in the trees and saw Wilt step out into the clearing. He was alone, with no sign of my bike.

Wilt walked to the middle of the clearing and stood in front of the full moon and near the single tree. He leaned his head back and called my name.

Rourk blew his duck call, and instantly Trevor and Teddy pulled the rope of sheets up. They ran forward and around Wilt as Aaron and Rourk made unsettling ghost noises. Wilt was so surprised he just stood there. In a couple of seconds, he was wrapped up to the tree.

I looked at Hairy and nodded. It was time for him to do his stuff. He pushed back his small sleeve and waved his wand. After chanting a few words, he levitated the sheet, and it floated up and out of the trees. It flitted toward Wilt like a hovering ghost and draped over his head.

Hairy climbed into my backpack, and I nervously stepped out of the trees and over to Wilt. I stood in front of him and in my deepest dad-sounding voice, asked...

Wilt started to apologize for a bunch of things he had done. He listed people he had pestered and stuff he had broken. I wasn't surpised by all the things he was saying, but I really just wanted my bike back. I asked him again where it was and he mumbled ...

IT'S IN THE MAINTENANCE SHOP NEXT TO MY HOUSE.

Still using my dad voice, I told my friends what to do.

They all answered back in their *best* grown-up voices.

I waved for Trevor to come with me, and the two of us raced through the trees and tombstones toward the back of the graveyard. The full moon was in front of us, and there were shooting stars flying through the sky.

The maintenance shop sat right next to Wilt's house. It was big and square with a small front door. I jiggled the knob, but it was locked. Looking up, I saw a small window above the door.

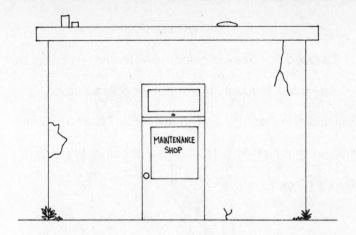

I pressed my face against the glass while Trevor shined a flashlight. There inside, leaning against the wall, was my bike.

I took off my backpack and unzipped it. Hairy popped out. Trevor was surprised to see him.

I put my backpack on and hoisted Hairy up.

Hairy pushed the top window, and it creaked open.

He pushed it some more and then began to crawl in.

Hairy slipped all the way in and dropped down to the floor. Trevor and I could *see* him jump up and grab the inside handle.

The door popped open, and we rushed in. Trevor flipped the flashlight back on, and I yanked the handlebars and flipped the bike around. I was wheeling it out the door when a porch light went on at Wilt's house, and there was the sound of someone yelling madly. My heart withered like a weed.

CHAPTER 12

ESCAPING

The yelling was coming from Wilt's mom and dad.
They had rushed out of their house and could see us
taking something from the maintenance shed. Trevor
turned off the flashlight just as Wilt's dad came
charging after us.

WHO'S OUT THERE?
WILT, IS THAT YOU?

I pushed my *bike* as *Trevor* scooped up Hairy. We shot toward the trees and tombstones with Wilt's dad chasing after us screaming . . .

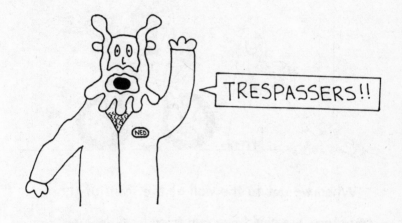

TRESPASSERS!!

We ran through the grass and gravestones back toward the clearing. I tried to get on my *bike* but my robe was in the way. When we reached the clearing, Wilt was no longer wrapped up, and there was no sign of the sheets or our friends. Trevor stopped to investigate. I yelled at him as I turned my head and shot my Nerf bow back behind us.

When we got to the wall at the front of the
cemetery, we could see our friends all looking over
and waving for us to hurry.

I didn't need to be told to run, I was already moving as quickly as I could. Trevor reached the wall first and scrambled up over it with Hairy. I would have done the same thing, but I had my bike. I lifted it up and Aaron reached over and yanked the other side.

Wilt's dad was getting closer and yelling things that didn't make a lot of sense.

As I climbed up onto the wall and tried to get over, the bottom of my robe snagged on something and made it so I couldn't move. I tugged and tugged, but it was caught hard. All my friends were too busy running away to notice I hadn't made it over.

Thanks to the knot I had tied on my belt, I couldn't slip out of my robe. I was in so much

trouble. I shut my eyes and imagined all the things
my parents were going to take away from me if I
actually got through this alive.

As I was imagining my awful fate, I felt Hairy climb
out of my backpack and crawl down my robe. I could
hear tearing and chewing, and in a few seconds, my
robe ripped and I was free. Hairy had chewed me
loose. I pulled myself all the way up onto the wall
and looked back. What I saw was pretty scary.

Wilt's dad had snagged Hairy! My mind raced as chapters from *Star Wars: A New Hope* consumed me. I couldn't leave Hairy. I was Han Solo, and he was my short wingman.

There was no way I could leave him behind. I
ripped off my torn bathrobe and threw it back over
the wall so it landed on Wilt's dad's head. I quickly
climbed over the wall and tried to wrestle Hairy
from his grip. I think Wilt's dad thought I was
some sort of spirit.

I made some scary sounds and pulled Hairy free.
Hairy clung to my neck as I picked up my backpack
and jumped the wall one last time. I fell hard onto

the dirt, jumped up, and grabbed my bike that was lying on the ground. Hairy climbed onto the top of my head, and I rode as fast as I could away from the cemetery and back home.

It was hard to tell which one of us sighed a bigger sigh of relief.

CHAPTER 13

AFTER MATH

Here's the good thing: once we got over that wall, nobody came chasing after us. I biked home without any other problem. My friends were all waiting on the island, where Jack explained what had happened.

WILT WAS CRYING LIKE A BABY. HE KEPT STRUGGLING, SO WE TOLD HIM WE'D LET HIM GO IF HE NEVER HARMED ANYONE AGAIN.

My friends had unwrapped Wilt. He thought they were all dads and ran away yelling for his mom. I couldn't believe it. We had done it! When I returned home, I was pretty scratched up and messy, but my parents didn't question me about it. They just thought I had been staring at the moon.

THERE'S OUR SCHOLAR.

At school the next day Wilt avoided all of us. In fact, he went out of his way to make sure no one saw him.

The news of what we had done traveled around the school like the wind. People I didn't even know started coming up to me in the halls and thanking me for whatever I had done to Wilt. It was like we had blown up the Death Star of bullies and now we were free.

As I walked out of my math class, I was stopped by Principal Smelt.

I know from experience that every time Principal Smelt wants to have a word with me, it's usually bad. Not that he's a mean principal; in fact, he's pretty interesting and very nice. Also, he plays the pan flute in what he calls a . . .

His progressive rock group is actually just him and some other old guy singing about things they think kids need or like. Their group is called Leftover Angst, and they perform at every assembly and school event we have. They write their own embarrassing songs. A couple of months ago, after a kid came to school with lice, they wrote a song about it and called a special assembly.

Principal Smelt cleared his throat and smiled. He then tugged at his mustache, which meant that he had good news. Of course, his version of good news was a lot different from mine. A couple of days ago, he had told me . . .

THEY'RE NOW MAKING LONG PANTS EVEN LONGER.

Like I said, he and I view good news differently. Today Principal Smelt told me that his progressive rock group had been invited to perform at the *Average Chef* tryouts tomorrow. I tried to look happy, but suddenly the tryouts didn't seem as cool as they once had. He told me how proud he was of me for being brave enough to, as he put it, "give it a go." He then added that he couldn't cheer for my team any louder than he could cheer for Janae's. He insisted that he needed to be an impartial cheerer and that, as principal of Softrock Middle School, he was required to like us all equally.

Principal Smelt had pulled out the gender sticks that he used when talking about the differences between boys and girls. The bell rang for my next class, but he just kept talking. He went on and on about how girls are important and began listing some of the things he thought women had invented.

Then, to be fair, he listed a few things that men might have invented. He didn't really have any idea what he was talking about, so he just went with things that sounded right.

I thanked him for the information and told him that I should probably get to class before I was marked tardy. I tried to pull away, but he had one last thing to say.

I just stood there in shock as Principal Smelt patted me on the back and went on and on about brotherhood. He felt I should include Tuffin in my cooking tryout because things like wars and hatred were caused by brothers not getting along.

I broke free and took off to class. I couldn't believe my mom had called my principal. There was no way I was going to include Tuffin now.

Before reaching my class, I ran into someone much prettier than Principal Smelt—Janae.

Janae was walking down the hall by herself. I thought it was a sign of how perfect we were for each other, us both being late to our classes. I could even *see* us as an old couple talking about it.

REMEMBER THAT ONE TIME WE WERE BOTH LATE TO CLASS?

NO.

Or maybe she was late because the vice principal had pulled her aside and told her she needed to include her sister in the tryouts. We both stopped a few feet away from each other. I knew I was supposed to be mad, and strong, and driven by the competition coming up, but Janae still made me weak in the neck.

I don't know why she made my whole body stop working. The two of us had known each other since we were little kids. We had even been through things like Imagination Camp together.

Ever since I had won the dramatic poetry contest, she had been extra nice to me at school. But now *Average Chef* was making everything more uncomfortable than ever. The whole reason I had wanted to try out was because I thought it would make Janae like me more. That was before I put my foot in my mouth and told her we would win.

Janae asked me if I was ready for the tryouts tomorrow, and in true nervous fashion, I replied...

YEPPY SMEPPY.

My face turned bright red, and Janae looked like I had just stepped down hard on her toes. I had no idea how to talk to girls. I was going to take off running, but she had something else to say.

OH, YEAH, YOUR MOM CALLED ME. SHE WANTED ME TO TELL YOU THAT YOU SHOULD INCLUDE YOUR LITTLE BROTHER.

I tried to move my lips to speak, but they just sort of flopped open and closed. Not only did I say dumb things like "yeppy smeppy," my mom was calling Janae and bothering her. Janae shook her head and walked off.

By the time I got to science, I was double tardy, and feeling triple dumb.

Right *before bed* that night, Libby came into my room to announce that she was going to sleep, so everyone needed to be extra quiet. I was playing Yo Mama with Hairy, which is just like Old Maid, but instead of calling the lady the Old Maid we call her Yo Mama.

YO MAMA

I didn't have a chance to hide Hairy before Libby barged in. She saw him on my floor holding cards, and gasped. Hairy just froze.

THAT'S THE UGLIEST STUFFED ANIMAL I'VE EVER SEEN.

I pushed Libby out of my room and then tried to calm Hairy down. He thought she was out of line telling people lies like that.

He finally cooled off and we finished our card game. We then spent the rest of the night reading cookbooks and trying to prepare for tomorrow.

CHAPTER 14

ONE LAST OBSTACLE

I woke up the next morning to the sound of Libby
screaming. Someone had snuck into her room and
mysteriously messed up all her makeup. I'm not
positive it was Hairy, but something about the way
he looked and spoke made me suspicious.

THAT TROLL
DESERVED IT.

I tried to explain to him that he had done a bad thing, *but he didn't understand.*

Hairy growled again, vowing to cast a spell on the troll himself as soon as he remembered a good one.

I probably would have *been* more interested in coming up with a spell that would cause Libby grief if I hadn't been so nervous about the tryouts this afternoon. There would be lights and cameras and lots of contestants. There would also be people from the show with microphones asking us questions.

Besides, I would be working with Jack and Teddy and Rourk and Aaron and Trevor. They still knew nothing about baking and making food, and only Aaron lied about having any skills.

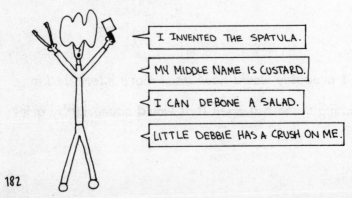

Aaron also called whisking "super stirring," and he thought broiling meant to roll things in nuts. The only real advantage we had was that all of us were incredibly average, and according to the name of the show, that was what was most important.

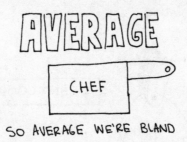

AVERAGE

CHEF

SO AVERAGE WE'RE BLAND

My friends came over to my house around noon for last-minute questions and one final pep talk. I tried to say things that would rally them and get them fired up for the competition.

THIS IS OUR TIME TO BAKE, OUR TIME TO SEAR!

Trevor looked slightly pumped up, and Jack called me a cooking nerd. The rest of my friends seemed too nervous to say anything. I knew none of them really wanted to do this, but they all felt obligated because of Janae and her friends challenging us. Jack kept insisting...

And I kept telling him that all he would have to do was just stand there and chop things or clean bowls. Rourk had other concerns.

I put my head in my hands and sighed. I had already told Rourk ten times that there would be no latex involved, but he still kept asking. Besides, he wasn't really allergic to latex—he was just scared of balloons.

Teddy was doing this for the dough.

HOW MUCH MONEY DOES THE WINNER GET?

They all knew that today was just the tryouts and that there was no money involved. I had told them a hundred times that if we won the tryouts, then we would be on the actual show and then maybe we might win ten thousand dollars.

Trevor started to lecture Jack about saving his money while the others argued over whether or not they should buy a solid gold car or a solid gold plane.

I couldn't think about any of that. I just wanted to make it through the day without looking worse in front of Janae. This wasn't supposed to be about selfish things like money or monkeys. This was supposed to be about me looking awesome in front of Janae.

To make things even more troublesome, my mom was gone doing something with Tuffin so she couldn't drive us to the tryouts. That meant my dad would have to do it. Don't get me wrong—I love my dad, but he drives like my grandma's great-grandma.

CAUTION IS COOL!

I don't think he's ever put the pedal to the metal. In fact, I don't think he's ever really pushed the gas pedal down. It always feels like we're crawling when he's at the wheel. Once, when I needed to get to the store to buy some shoes that were on sale, he drove so slow that by the time we got there I was out of luck.

So it made me uneasy to know that we were going to be dependent on my father to get us to the tryouts on time. The rules to the competition clearly stated that any team that wasn't there by the start time was automatically eliminated.

I grabbed my backpack and my recipes, and we all loaded into our huge van. My dad pulled out of the driveway and began to drive in the wrong direction. I knew the Civic Center was near the small hills, and we were heading away from them.

My heart passed out. I hated my dad's quick stops—they were never quick. In fact, his quick stops were a big reason he was always late.

I couldn't talk my dad out of his quick stop, no matter how hard I tried. He needed to drop off a swing at a park on the other side of town. One of their swings was broken, and he had promised to deliver a new one today. I begged and pleaded with him to go to the tryouts first, but he kept saying . . .

When we arrived at the park, my dad got out his toolbox and took off the broken swing. He then attached the new one and asked me to test the swing to make sure it worked.

By the time we got back into the van, there were only twenty-five minutes until the tryouts started, and we were at least twenty-six minutes away. Even Jack was growing anxious.

Despite being in a hurry, my dad drove five miles under the speed limit while whistling. Also, every school zone we went through, he slowed down even more. I rubbed my eyes out of frustration. It was Saturday, and the schools weren't even in session, but he insisted on going slow anyway.

I glanced at the clock on the dashboard and moaned. The tryouts started in ten minutes, and we were at least fifteen minutes away. Trevor suggested we all cry to make my dad go faster. It wasn't the best plan, but it was all we had. But our wailing and complaining didn't seem to faze my father in the least.

He just kept whistling and talking as if there was no urgency at all.

DID I EVER TELL YOU BOYS ABOUT THE TIME I SAT AND DID NOTHING FOR HOURS?

My dad stopped the car completely while we waited for a train to cross in front of us. I was thinking about pulling my hair out when I felt something tap my right foot. I looked down, and there, peeking out of my backpack, was Hairy. I had brought him only because he had promised to stay hidden. I motioned for him to get back in, but instead of listening, he pulled out his right hand and lifted up his wand. He pointed it toward my dad's head and mumbled something. Strong red sparks flew out of the end of the wand, and instantly my dad's glasses fogged up.

HEY, I CAN'T SEE A THING!

I looked at Hairy and panicked. I wasn't sure how my dad being blind would help the situation. To make things scarier, all the van windows began to fog up too. The van grew dark, and there was no sign of an outside world. I could feel my seat rock and then, with a swift forward motion, I felt the entire van being lifted. My body pressed back into my seat as the vehicle lunged forward. Everyone was screaming and crying for real now.

My dad seemed oblivious to it all. He took off his glasses and was wiping the lenses with his tie. Since he couldn't see very well with his glasses off, he didn't even notice the fogged-up windows or the fact that we seemed to be flying—which was weird, because it felt like we were soaring miles above the earth.

A few seconds later, we could feel the van drop and touch the ground. We all bounced in our seat belts as the vehicle came to a sudden stop. Instantly the windows cleared up, and I could see that we were parked out in front of the civic center. My dad finished cleaning his glasses and put them back on.

My friends and I caught our breath. I looked
down at Hairy as he slipped back into my pack. I
felt sick, exhilarated, and nervous all at the same
time. Part of me had been hoping to be late and be
disqualified so I wouldn't have the chance to fail.

We all stumbled out of the van and into the Civic
Center.

CHAPTER 15

—

ABOVE AVERAGE

Inside the civic center, everybody was running around. The noise was as loud as when my sister blow-dries her hair and sings with the radio turned up.

HOLDING...

SODA...

HOLDING HANDS AND DRINKING SODA...

We checked in thirteen seconds before the cutoff time. Following that, a lady with tall black hair gave us all name tags and showed us on a map where we would be stationed.

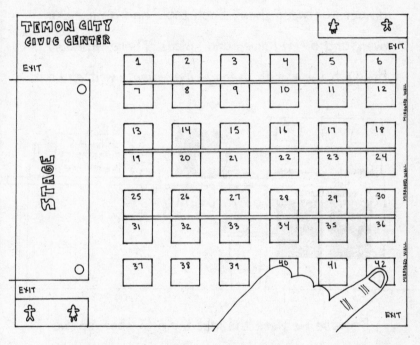

The tryouts were being held in a huge room that had mirrors on the far wall and large buzzing lights hanging from the ceiling. At the front of the room was a stage with two potted plants on it. I could see

197

Principal Smelt and his band setting up on the left side of the stage near the bathrooms.

There were a lot of other teams participating in the tryouts, and the tables were lined up in rows with dividers between them. Each table had a mixer, an oven, and a few knives and spices. There was also a box with the words *average ingredients* written on it.

Because we were the last team to show up, we were put at the last table in the far corner. Janae and her team were right across the aisle at station 36. Janae was there with five other girls. Three of the girls were the Dodge triplets—Pixie, Patsy, and Petra.

I had never really gotten along with the triplets. They were cranky and always together. Whenever they walked down the halls at school, they held hands and wouldn't get out of anyone's way. I've been shoved up against the lockers more than once by them squeezing me to the side.

EXCUSE YOU!

Not only were the Dodge triplets cranky, but their dad owned a catering business, so they probably were pretty good cooks. Janae's team had matching aprons and rubber gloves. There was even a banner on the front of their table with their chosen team name.

#36 AVERAGE CUTIES

Both our tables were at the far end of the room near the mirrored wall. Music started to play, and everyone began to clap as the host of *Average Chef*, Chad Average, walked up onto the stage. The stage was so far away from us that we couldn't really see. Luckily, there were TVs we could watch on the walls in the back. Chad Average waited for the clapping to stop and then shouted . . .

WHO HERE'S AVERAGE?

I thought all my friends knew what to shout...

My friends stared at me like I was crazy. Chad Average clapped and then held his hands up to quiet all the tables. He told us we had one hour to make the best food we could, using the eight average ingredients in our boxes. At the end of the hour, a judge would taste our meal. The two highest-scoring teams would be featured on the *Average Chef* TV show in two weeks.

The contestants put their hands on the top of their boxes and counted down with him. I then lifted the lid, and we all looked in.

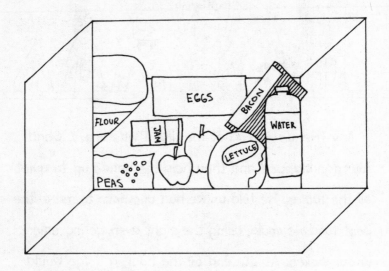

The ingredients were simple and every table had the same ones. There were no real surprises in the box. I was already thinking of a few things we could make. But before we could start, we needed to know which of the eight average items we were supposed to focus on. I was hoping it would be the bacon, but I was wrong.

There was a huge groan from everyone in the room. Water was the most boring item in the box. There was no way to make water anything but plain. Rourk had a suggestion.

As much as I could see the wisdom in what he was saying, I wasn't going to quit and let Janae and her team beat us.

LOOK ON THE BRIGHT SIDE—NO LATEX.

The host shouted, "Let's all aim for average," and then rang a bell. The competition was on. Everyone around us instantly began to chop and wash food as Principal Smelt and his band started to play music.

It was lame, but it was probably one of their best songs. I opened my backpack to get my recipes, and there was Hairy, smiling and waving his wand.

I had no time to mess with him, so I told him to keep quiet, grabbed my recipe cards, and zipped him back in. I flipped through the cards and found two recipes that I thought we could use—a soup and a salad. We didn't have all the ingredients, but I figured with some creativity, we could make them work. Everyone seemed okay with my choices.

Teddy crushed up crackers. Rourk sifted flour. Aaron took the apples and started to peel them while Jack worked on chopping up some lettuce. Trevor and I mixed flour and egg together and created some dough. Time was flying, and after twenty minutes, all we had were some piles of chopped things and a wad of sticky dough.

I looked over at Janae's table. She and her team were whisking and measuring like they were food fairies. Everything looked so peaceful and happy at their table.

I threw some croutons in the oven to bake, then began mixing some of the chopped food together. A lady with a microphone and big teeth stopped by our table and began to ask questions. The microphone seemed to make us all nervous, so we just stood there smiling.

The big-toothed lady tried asking another question. We just kept smiling. Only Aaron found the courage to speak up. Of course, he didn't really answer the question.

DO YOU KNOW WHERE THE BATHROOM IS?

The lady didn't look too impressed with us. She left and went to talk to Janae's table.

I put my head down, and we all kept on working. Before I knew it, an alarm rang announcing that there were only ten minutes left.

THERE'S NO WAY WE'LL MAKE IT!

I pulled out two plates and set them on the table. I then looked at the oven. The croutons I was baking weren't quite done, and the bacon on the stove was still way undercooked.

The room *seemed* to sway and then come to a
complete *stop*. Then everything froze, and there was
no longer any *sound*. The question lady was frozen
mid-stride, and I could *see* pepper and other
ingredients floating in the air. I *seemed* to be the
only thing moving. I looked around, and Hairy
popped up on the table waving his wand and smiling.

Somehow Hairy had stopped time; his spells were getting so much stronger. The only noise now was the sound of our bacon frying. Everything except for me, Hairy, and what I was cooking remained frozen.

I wanted to be excited, but I knew there was probably some rule about contestants not being allowed to stop time. I looked at Janae's team. They were all frozen.

I stared at the mirrored wall next to us, and for some magical reason, my reflection was doing something odd in the mirror. It looked like I was walking over to Janae and dumping a huge pile of salt into the food she was making. I wasn't actually doing it, but the mirror seemed to be showing me what I wanted to do.

It was just like the mirror of Erised at the end of *Harry Potter.* I looked down at the salt shaker on my table. I picked it up and thought about how easy it would be to ruin the food Janae and her team were making. The problem was I liked Janae way more than I wanted to win this stupid cooking contest. There was just no way I could do that to her. I set the salt shaker down and sighed. My reflection seemed mad at me for chickening out.

Hairy spotted his own reflection, and the Chewbacca part of him started snarling. He growled at himself

and then ran as fast as he could, slamming up against
his own reflection.

As Hairy fell to the ground, his wand sparked,
and like a film speeding up, time began to move
again. I grabbed Hairy and shoved him back into my
pack and then stood up and tried to look innocent.
The bacon in my pan was now perfectly cooked, and
the croutons were done. I was going to spend more
time marveling over what had happened, but I was
interrupted by Chad Average announcing...

My friends and I began throwing things together. I took the croutons out and pulled the bacon from the stovetop. We put some of the chopped lettuce in a row, and Trevor tried to shape it like a big piece of bacon while I put some chopped apples and bacon in a bowl and poured water over it.

Teddy mixed some gelatin with water, and we dripped it over the salad as Rourk and Aaron made a decorative ring of jam around the soup bowl while Trevor added pieces of fried egg to the apple, bacon bits, water soup. Jack was in charge of the silverware and he had forgotten it. He started freaking out about us missing our spoons and forks, so I had to calm him down.

Jack actually smiled and came up with a solution with only two seconds to spare.

We all threw our hands up. I looked at our plates and thought we just might have a chance. I was pretty certain what we had made didn't taste great, but it looked okay.

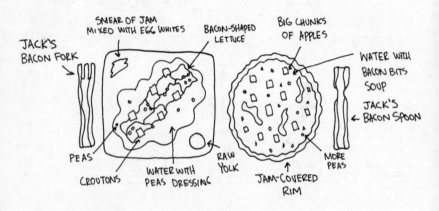

We glanced over to see what Janae and her friends had made. I don't want to sound braggy, but ours looked way better. In fact, it looked like they hadn't finished. One of their plates was okay, but the other one only had peas on it.

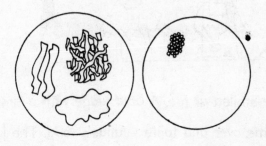

I glanced at Janae as she stood there frowning. She looked at her food and sighed. I felt bad for her. I was extra glad I hadn't dumped that salt on her food. Jack pointed at their practically empty plate.

I don't know why I did what I did next. I mean, it was a competition, and I wasn't supposed to talk to the enemy, yet for some reason my legs started to move without my permission. I walked out from behind our table and up to Janae's. The triplets growled at me as I congratulated Janae.

Janae smiled at me. A bald judge with a tiny
nose came over and tasted Janae's food. The judge
seemed to like it, but then marked them down
because they were missing part of their meal.

The bald judge then came to our table and tasted
ours. I'm not positive, but I don't think he liked
what we made.

He called our food disgusting, bland, and chewy before running off. We then stood around until it was time for the results. After all the tables had been judged, Chad Average walked back up onto the stage to announce the two winning teams. The first team to win was a table of women who were all wearing red hats. They had made bread boats in jam and swamp water salad.

I personally think the red-hat ladies cheered louder than was necessary. It took a while for Chad Average to calm them down. Once they finally left the stage, Chad read off the second and final winner.

AND OUR FINAL AVERAGE TEAM IS... TEAM BURNSIDE!

I couldn't believe they had called my name. I thought after the way the judge had gagged and run off, that we didn't have a chance. I looked at my friends. All of them seemed equally confused. Trevor's eyes widened, and he pointed toward the stage. I was so shocked by what I saw that my mouth dropped and all my fingers fell to the floor.

It wasn't me that had won. It was a different

Burnside.

CONGRATULATIONS

Tuffin and my mom were the second winning

team. I had no clue they were even in the contest.

They had been at station 3. My mom had gladly included Tuffin on her team. In fact, it was Tuffin's ideas that had won it for them.

WATERFALL SPAGHETTI

PEAS IN POOL

I wanted to be mad, but for some reason, I was proud of Tuffin. I figured if it couldn't be me that people adored, it might as well be my little brother. Everyone clapped wildly as they put a chef's hat on Tuffin and knighted him with a spatula.

FROM THIS DAY FORTH, YOU SHALL BE KNOWN AS SIR AVERAGE.

I never found out if our food was any good, because by the time I finished congratulating Tuffin, Rourk had eaten it.

YOU ATE IT ALL?

WHAT? I DIDN'T WANT IT TO GO TO WASTE.

Rourk actually did us all a favor. By the time we got home, he was so sick from what we had made that he couldn't go out for "congratulations" and "nice try" ice cream with the rest of us.

I THINK I NEED TO BE NEAR MY BATHROOM.

We all tried to act sad, but it sort of served Rourk right, seeing as how he had eaten all the food. Plus, we all knew how much more ice cream there would be for each of us without him there to hog it.

CHAPTER 16

OPEN

Two weeks later, Tuffin and my mom went on TV and competed against the ladies in the red hats. Tuffin didn't win, but he had a great time, and unlike his older brother, he was nice enough to let me be on his team. I even got to be on TV when they filmed me chopping onions.

It wasn't my proudest moment, but it was cool. I hate to say it, but I just might have learned something from the whole Average Chef/Tuffin thing. I'm not sure what I learned, but I feel smarter. My dad said I'm...

...CHANGING FROM A LITTLE MAN TO A MEDIUM MAN.

I don't know if it was Hairy or just the books I've been reading, but my life is much more interesting than it used to be.

In the two weeks since the competition, I've pretty much spent all my time with Hairy. If Trevor is over, we all talk about spells and Han Solo. And when it's just me and Hairy, we read.

I've grown *so* close to Hairy that I hardly think about Wonkenstein. Every once in a while, I look at Wonk's cane on my dresser or I eat a piece of candy and think about him, but Hairy really has all my attention now. I've even taken him with me to school a couple of times. The first time went fine, but the second time, I almost got caught when Hairy spotted Wilt and did a spell . . .

I had to quickly explain that Wilt was acting okay now. Hairy then changed him back. Since that day, I've not brought Hairy to school. Besides, his spells are getting stronger and stronger, and I'm sort of afraid of what could happen.

Yesterday Janae sat two seats down from me at lunch. I made a joke about school food, and she actually laughed. I then smiled without making a fool of myself. It was a great lunch, despite the food.

Thursday evening after dinner, I went straight to my room and took Hairy from the drawer. I started reading him a part of *Harry Potter* that I enjoyed. Right as we were getting to a really scary scene, something even scarier happened.

I nearly jumped out of my skin.

AHHHH!!

My closet door had knocked again. The last time that happened, Wonkenstein had gone in and never come back out. I looked down at Hairy, and he was smiling and moving toward the closet as if he had been waiting for the knock.

OH, NO YOU DON'T, BOOKFRIEND!

I picked him up and put him on my bed. I then continued to read as if nothing had happened.

My heart felt like it was going to burst. I wasn't going to let Hairy disappear back into my closet. I held his scarf as he struggled to break loose and get to the closet.

Beardy began to rattle and shake.

Then, with one loud snap, the closet door popped

open.

TELL DUMBLEDORE AND HAN THAT I'LL BE FINE.

WHAT DOES THAT MEAN?

IT MEANS GOOD-BYE!

I jumped up and quickly pushed my closet door

closed. It growled and popped back open. I pushed

it closed again, and this time, I leaned against it with

my rear to keep it closed. Beardy bit my backside,

and I leapt away. The door rumbled and then flung

open. Hairy started to walk toward it, and I scooped

him up. I opened my front window and crawled out of

it, taking Hairy away from my room. I scurried across my front yard and over to the island. I held Hairy tightly and sat down between the palm trees near the Flinger.

I looked at my house and at my open window. I could see my closet door. It was opening and closing as if champing to get at Hairy.

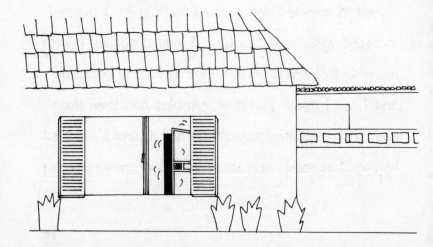

My mind raced. I tried to think of something about Chewbacca or Harry Potter that the books had taught me. Some sort of spell or secret hold that would keep Hairy still. I couldn't think of anything. Hairy tossed his head back and hit my chin. I yelled, and he slipped out of my grasp. He turned to face me and spoke his mixed-up wisdom.

DON'T WORRY, ROB. WHAT IS NOW MIGHT SEEM WONDERFUL, BUT THERE IS FAR MORE MAGIC JUST AROUND THE CORNER.

I stared at Hairy, wondering what he meant. I didn't know what was now, and I couldn't see any corners. I begged him to please stop trying to sound wise. Hairy patted my right knee and told me this was just the beginning. I reached out to grab him and stopped.

He nodded at me, and I nodded back as if I understood. But I wouldn't stand for it. He lifted his wand and shouted, "Accio brooms." The front doors of all the homes around us instantly popped open. Brooms of all shapes and sizes shot out of the doors and flew across the street toward the island.

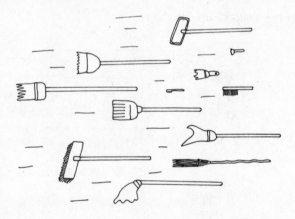

Hairy was summoning a ride. Brooms pummeled us from all directions. I jumped up and frantically tried to grab as many as possible to keep Hairy from getting them. I had most of them, but when I looked down, I could see that he had thought of another way to travel.

He was standing on the far edge of the Flinger, and there was a huge rock levitating above the near end. Hairy waved his wand and let the rock fall. I dropped the brooms and leapt toward him, but I was too slow. He shot across the street, right through my window and directly into my closet. I then heard the door shut loudly.

SLAM!!

I ran across the street and climbed into my window. My closet door was closed, but it wasn't locked. I threw the door open, and there was nothing but junk.

I turned around to see if by some chance Hairy was in my room. I checked to make sure he hadn't crawled into his drawer. He hadn't. When I turned and tried to look in the closet again, it was shut tight, and Beardy wasn't budging.

I felt mad, sad, and confused all at once. I could hear knocking on the front door of our house. I ran out of my room, hoping someone had found Hairy and brought him back.

IF FOUND PLEASE CALL ROB
@
555-5464
CAUTION: HE MAY BITE.

When I got to the front door, there was Trevor's mom. She was complaining to my mom and holding a bunch of brooms. She didn't look happy.

Trevor's mom had seen me with them on the island. I started to explain, but it was hard to come up with a believable reason.

It was probably the worst excuse I could have used. My mom was pretty angry. In fact, she called me Robert instead of Ribert and then assigned me a number of new jobs that would keep me cleaning for the next few weeks. I walked back into my room and shut the door. I looked over at Beardy, and he was smiling.

Beardy appeared to be looking down.

I looked down, too. There was something lying on the floor near the closet door.

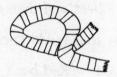

I smiled and picked up the little scarf. I then folded it carefully and put it on the top of my dresser next to Wonk's cane.

I looked back at Beardy and asked...

Beardy didn't answer; instead, I heard a knock on my window. I turned to see all my friends staring at me. I opened the window, and Jack spoke up.

WE FOUND A BOX OF WOMEN'S SHOES IN THE ALLEY, AND WE'RE GONNA FLING 'EM. WANNA COME?

It was an offer I couldn't refuse.

ACKNOWLEDGMENTS

Sometimes people do things that are worth mentioning.
One time I found a twenty-dollar bill and gave it to
someone who claimed it was theirs. Does that make me
a hero? Who's to say, but at the very least it's worth
mentioning. There are those who have played a big role in
making this series what it is. And those people are not
only worth mentioning, they are worth going on and on
about. But for the sake of time and space, I'll simply
mention them and then go on.

So here's to Bennett, Missy, Naomi, Mark, Jon, Liz,
Aunt Lee, Amy, Mary, Nina, Kindred, Archie, Nero,
Roald, Diane, Charlie, Grant, Byron, Karen, Matt, 2152,
Ben, Jasper, Adam, Joe, Morrissey, Phoebe, George,
Scott, Tim, Aaron, Sam, East, LeeAnne, Matt, Julie,

Bobby, David, Mikey, Jeffy, Grandpa, Grandma, Chris, E.B., Jack, Curry, Billy, Doug, Iris, Matilda, Henry V, Santiago, Wolfe, Clark, my amazing dad, Roark, Trevor, Golf, Travis, Brian, Kevin, Jenny, Julie, Dottie, Teddy, Martin, Fred, Avenue, and Exerplay. Thank you all.

I would be remiss and remorseful if I didn't mention the amazing people at Henry Holt/Macmillan. It's a privilege to work with all of you.

Laurie thanks for putting this book in the right hands. Grateful is a word I do not use lightly. So, let me drop it like a weight. I am so grateful for all that you've done.

Let me add, none of this would have been possible, or any fun, without my phenomenal editor and friend, Christy. Everything good about this series is because of you. I think Albert Finney sang it best, "Thank you very much, thank you very much . . ."

And finally, Krista. What's the deal? How could one person have so much patience and kindness? It's hard to imagine anything worthwhile without you.

BONUS MATERIALS

GOFISH

OBERT SKYE

What sparked your imagination for *Potterwookie*?
My imagination is always in overdrive. I think one of the reasons for this is because so many books have made my mind a playground of ideas and possibilities. The thought for *Potterwookiee* came a long time ago when I first saw *Star Wars*. I wanted to be Chewbacca. He was cool, tall, and funny. So when it came time to enter Rob's closet for a second time, I KNEW it was time for CHEW.

Which character in the book do you think you are most like? Whom do you most relate to?
I think I most relate to Rob. In middle school, my life was sort of a mess. I didn't always feel like I fit in or said the right things. I like how Rob makes mistakes, but he always tries to find a way to fix them. I also relate to Hairy. I wish I was that cool and magical. And I want my own wand.

If you heard a strange rattling sound in your closet and discovered a mythical creature there, what's the first thing you would do?
Duck behind my bed and scream. Actually, I'd probably scream and then duck.

What scenes were your favorite to write?

There are so many scenes in *Potterwookie* that I loved writing. I like when they are flinging things with the Flinger. I love when Hairy is wearing the baseball-cap sorting-hat. Oh, I also like when they go on a slow-speed car chase through school zones. Plus, I enjoy the food they make near the end. There are more things I love, but I'll leave it to readers to determine what parts are the best.

Who is your favorite fictional character and why?

Willy Wonka. I like how odd he is and that he owns a chocolate factory. My goal is to have my own chocolate factory someday. I want to be like Willy.

Why did you choose to cross Harry Potter and Chewbacca from *Star Wars*? Are you a big fan of *Star Wars*? Harry Potter?

I am a huge *Star Wars* fan and a massive Harry Potter fanatic. Of all the books and ideas that have inspired me growing up, these two series did the most. They took me to the coolest places and delivered the best stories. Combining the two was a natural fit. Who doesn't want a Potterwookiee? I know I do.

Who or what did you most like to doodle when you were young?

I liked to doodle everything. Weird animals were my favorite subjects. I did a comic strip for my school called *Prep-punker*. It was about a goofy, preppy punk rocker. It was kind of my beginning telling stories with pictures.

What kind of books did you enjoy most when you were young?

I loved anything funny and exciting. Those were my two

favorite types of books to read then and now. I loved when a book made me laugh and caused my heart to beat fast. I always try to make my books have a lot of humor and exciting things happening in them.

Can you tell us a little about what to expect in *Pinocula*? (No spoilers, please!)
When the closet opens again, you are in for a great surprise. There is something very fun about a little lying wooden vampire. I love how much trouble he gets into and how Rob has to deal with the aftermath. It's a story that bites and rules at the same time.

Meet Pinocula, the new creature
from Rob's closet. He is a liar and a jokester
and is determined to drive Rob crazy.

What do you get when you
combine Pinocchio with Dracula?

Keep reading for a sneak peek!

THE STARTING LIE

Since my time machine didn't work, I was forced to go to school today, and here's what happened. After lunch we had a school assembly. The speaker was a Temon city worker with poofy hair. He came to talk to us about his job working at the city parks. He talked a lot about watering things. He went on and on about how challenging his work was and then he said . . .

EVERY DAY, I COME HOME POOPED FROM DOING MY DUTY.

I didn't want to laugh, but I couldn't help it—words like *duty* and *pooped* are immaturity power words. The second I laughed, the whole crowd began to laugh with me. It took Principal Smelt ten minutes to get everyone calmed down, and Mr. Poofy Hair stormed off the stage in a huff. I shouldn't have laughed, but city workers need to be careful about what they say in front of middle schoolers.

I was raised not to joke about gross things. When I was really little, my mom made me watch *The Adventures of Bathroom Billy.* It's an educational show about a talking toilet named Billy that helps kids know how to properly act in the bathroom.

I had failed Bathroom Billy, and my laughing had ruined the whole assembly. The speaker was mad, the teachers were mad, and lots of the students were mad because we had to go back to our classes. Principal Smelt was so upset his ears were steaming. As I was walking out of the assembly, he stopped me in the hall to ask me if I had anything to do with what he was calling...

THE GREAT ASSEMBLY DISASTER!

Principal Smelt was angrier than I had ever seen him before. His face was red, and his mustache looked sweaty. He wanted me to name names. He wanted me to tell him everyone I had seen laughing.

He also informed me that the city worker with the poofy hair was actually his second cousin.

I felt bad, but I also felt like I should keep my mouth shut. I didn't *see* how it would help for me to speak up and let him know it was my fault. Principal Smelt wiped his forehead and asked,

Okay, this is the spot where I need to remind you that I've already apologized. I shouldn't have laughed at what my principal's second cousin had said, but I especially shouldn't have opened my mouth and lied about it.

IT DEFINITELY WASN'T ME.

Principal Smelt stared at my swelling nose for a moment. He sighed louder than anyone I had ever heard sigh before and then smiled weakly. He patted me on the shoulder and called me a good egg.

I'M GOOD.

Principal Smelt concluded our conversation by informing me that he needed to find and punish the students who laughed first. He assigned me to do some "sleuthing" and discover who the "instigator" was. I said okay, even though I didn't completely understand what he was asking.

So, after dinner tonight, I looked up the word *instigator* in my mom's old dictionary. According to the definition, I was one. I had instigated the laughing, and I followed that laughing by lying. Principal Smelt was wrong—I was a *bad* egg.

I'M OOZING.

I sat down on my bed and stared at my closet door. Beardy, the little face on my brass closet doorknob, looked like he was disappointed in me.

Beardy made me think of Wonkenstein and Hairy. I missed the first two creatures that had come out of my closet. It'd be great to have them here now so that I could explain myself to somebody.

Wonk and Hairy had made my life pretty crazy, but they had been fun to have around. Not a day went by when I didn't wish they'd at least return for a visit. I've tried to get back into my closet to see if anyone else might be in there, but Beardy keeps it locked tight.

I wanted to lie down on my bed and rest, but the word *lie* made me uncomfortable. I opened my bedroom window to climb out and go see my friends. As I was climbing out, I heard a scratching noise coming from behind my closet door. I spun around. My closet gurgled and burped loudly. Light began to seep out from beneath the door. To make things more unsettling, Beardy was shining.

I reached out to turn Beardy. He was locked and hot, causing me to yelp. I stepped back and stared at my closet door. My insides tumbled and turned like grapes in a washing machine.